SLEEPERS AWAKE

Winner of the Eludia Award

Hidden River Arts offers the Eludia Award for a first book-length unpublished novel or collection of stories by a woman writer, age 40 or above. The Eludia Award provides $1000 and publication by Hidden River Publishing on its Sowilo Press imprint. The purpose of the prize is to support the many women writers who meet with delays and obstacles in discovering their creative selves.

Hidden River Arts is an interdisciplinary arts organization dedicated to supporting and celebrating the unserved artists among us, particularly those outside the artistic and academic mainstream.

ALSO BY TREE RIESENER

Liminalog
Angel Poison
Inscapes
EK: Poems of Ekphrasis (FORTHCOMING)
The Hubble Cantos (FORTHCOMING)

Sleepers Awake

◈ Stories ◈

TREE RIESENER

S SOWILO PRESS • *Philadelphia 2015*

The author gratefully thanks these magazines and organizations that have published, recognized, or presented in a public forum the following stories:

"Airdwellers" in *NEBO: A Literary Journal*; "The BVM" in *Writing Aloud*, InterAct Theatre, Philadelphia; "Demon Love Story" in *Identity Theory*; "Diary" (First Prize, Philadelphia Writers Conference) in *Wigleaf*; "Hungry" in *Flash Fiction Online*; "Modems to Hell" in *Hinge*; "On the C Bus" in *Writing Aloud*, InterAct Theatre, Philadelphia; "Sleepers Awake" in *Istanbul Literary Review*; "Who Do You Say I Am?" in *Evergreen Review*.

Library of Congress Control Number: 2015947693
ISBN 978-0-9844727-5-8

SOWILO PRESS
An imprint of Hidden River Publishing
Philadelphia, Pennsylvania

for those I love

Contents

SLEEPERS AWAKE

Losing St. Augustine

Spring

If you've been in love, you know that impulse to give your love object anything you've got.

So to show Joanie how much I loved her, I gave her the secret of my success—a little cinder, the saintly equivalent of the tooth fairy, my relic, a first-class one, the actual body part, the last surviving (or at least last known outside the Vatican) ashy fragment of St. Augustine on earth.

She lost it.

"What do you mean, you lost it? You can't have lost it? Somewhere in your apartment, right?"

Sounding like it was a joke, she told me in that innocent, it isn't-really-important-is-it sweet little voice, big blue eyes wide open in doe-like innocence, "I don't think so. I had it in my pocket. When I got home, it wasn't there. I'm *sorry.*"

Then *I* lost it.

"You're sorry? You're *sorry*? That was a sacred relic, a remnant of one of Christendom's holiest saints. You don't shove something like that in your pocket. You take care of it. Put it in your purse at least. If I gave you a fragment of the true cross, what would you do? Use it for a toothpick?"

I screamed at her until I felt asthma coming on and snapped the phone shut. God, sometimes you really wish we still had receivers to slam down. When she kept calling and calling, I turned the ringtone off.

That piece of the rock, a little chunk about the size and shape of a lima bean, had been with me all through college. I carried it in my pocket when I went on the interview that landed me my first job. Even now, before I did anything hard, like take a chance on some insider trading, I'd feel in my pocket to make sure that little lump was there. How was I going to be audacious without it? And if I wasn't audacious, who was I?

I put it under my pillow when I slept. If I was going out partying and thought I might get a little wasted, I did what any caretaker would do, left him safe in a bottle of Laphroig single-malt, his usual home when he wasn't doing anything else. Tequila drinkers have their little worm at the bottom of the bottle. I had St. Augustine in mine. Every time I took a drink, I imbibed a bit of the old saint.

I got the idea from when I'd been a classics major, before I decided to go over to business. A queen of antiquity, Artemisia, did the same thing for her husband, Mausoleus, when she drank his ashes in wine, over time making herself his tomb, from which we get—you got it—the word mausoleum. Talk about your romantic ideas. . . . Am I right?

Anyway, the human body is completely replaced after seven years so I thought after seven, my DNA would have been transformed into Augustine's. Sort of. I'm not saying I would have his mind or soul. Just the body. I thought I could build on that, the mind-body continuum thing, and I totally credit it for helping me to overcome my natural shyness, and I think giving me the edge when I took the GMAT, considering my grade-point average was pretty average.

I'd got him on the internet, ten years ago, the summer before I started college, with the money from my job as a waiter at the Olive Garden, from a priest who was selling relics on eBay. I wasn't naive, checked him out.

He was for real, a Jesuit no less. The Jesuits, they're sort of the free agents of the church. They know how to get stuff like that. This guy probably had a basement full of body parts and a gambling problem. At any rate, my certificate of authenticity with a red wax seal assured me I'd got the last bit of St. Augustine on the open market, and now that I didn't have him with me anymore, I felt naked.

I'd told Joanie the story that night I gave him to her as a place holder for an engagement ring. I was crazy in love and wanted to give her my most precious thing.

"I'll redeem him with a diamond as soon as we find one you like. Think of yourself as a pretty kidnapper holding a saint, no less, for ransom."

In my happiness, I joked around a little, but I thought she'd been with me long enough to know how I felt about him. She'd been brought up Pentecostal, but she'd put that behind her when she bought her first pair of Jimmy Choo shoes and now didn't give much of a damn about anything in the religion line. She was perfectly willing to go along with any denominational choice I made, and she only teased me a little about my piece of the rock.

After the engagement kiss, I'd put him in her hand and folded her fingers up over him. It had been incredibly meaningful to me. Her? She hadn't kept him even twenty-four hours, hadn't even managed to keep him between her place and mine, and now he was just part of the anonymous dust of New York City.

After the terrible pain of the first twenty-four hours of losing her and losing St. Augustine, the more I thought about her, the more her faults appeared. Maybe this had been Augustine's way of looking out for me, his last kindness. The way she just kicked her Jimmy Choos off and left them in the living room. The way she always had cat hair on her Vera Wang sweaters. The way she wrote reminders on her hand like a grubby middle school girl in a gym tunic with a field hockey stick instead of digging into her Prada bag for the Mont Blanc pen and expensive Clairefontaine memo book I'd given her.

On the other hand, Augustine and I had been together a long time. I felt the way conjoined twins must feel when they're separated. I tried to cheer up. Maybe that was a good analogy. I hadn't lost him. We were just undergoing a separation, sort of like we were at different colleges. We were on a break. He might show up again. One of these days I'd be walking down the street, and a little chunk of rock in a vacant lot would call to me.

I started talking to him a lot in my mind, out loud when I was alone. That helped, but there was definitely a void when I was on the trading floor thinking what I should do in the hysteria all around me, and I'd put my hand in my pocket for some guidance and nothing was there.

Then one evening a couple of weeks later, I was steaming up the windows of my apartment with boiling water to make spaghetti puttanesca, and she called. Without looking at the caller screen, I answered and heard her lilting voice full of bells, a little uncertain now.

"Please don't hang up. Guess what? I found St. Augustine. He'd slipped through a hole in the lining of my pocket."

I felt a little suspicious. It was all so pat, but I said she could come over.

As soon as she came in the door, she put the little chunk in my hand. It looked the same.

"Are you sure this is it? You didn't ring in some substitute? Pick up a piece of rock on the street?"

"You think I would do something like that? I swear to God!"

It didn't escape me that she hadn't exactly answered the question, but the chunk looked like Augustine and she looked so sweet I decided to go for it. After all, the proof of the pudding is in the eating.

I thought I'd start out by giving him a try, put him in the spaghetti sauce while it cooked and then rinsed him off and put him on the kitchen window sill.

After we ate, we sat together and watched some sitcom re-runs—you can't help thinking what Will and Grace would do with Sodom and Gomorrah—and then, I couldn't help it, I loved her, we went to bed and it was like it always was. Better. If the truth be told, I felt Augustine was right there with me, and we went for it time after time. I remembered his famous young man's prayer, Lord, make me good, but not yet. I was convinced it was the real chunk.

I tend to forget everybody's not up on all the facts about Augustine, but he's regarded as one of the greatest thinkers of all time although, and I quote, he had a "morally and doctrinally disordered youth" until he met St. Ambrose and got converted. It's the part about being morally and doctrinally disordered that's always made me feel close to him.

It wasn't long before everything I touched turned to gold. I was trading on the floor and pretty soon I had a piece of the Trump, a Lamborghini, a small but choice art collection and a beautiful bride. As time went on, the only thing that was lacking was a child. Eventually, we made the preliminary inquiries into fertility treatment.

Just in case it might be me, I tried to put the saint into something I ate or drank every day. Morning coffee. Evening brandy. When he wasn't swimming in my bottle of scotch, he had his special place on a little Chinese saucer on the kitchen window sill where the sun splashed in for his vitamin D.

After a while, I started to worry.

"Do you think Augustine's smaller than he used to be?"

After all, maybe the man looked like a little chunk of rock but he wasn't. Just petrified saint. He still felt as hard as ever but was it possible I was washing little bits of him away? Maybe that was why we hadn't conceived yet. He was getting weaker.

I started to ration him out, didn't put him in everything I ate or drank anymore, didn't put him in the bottle of scotch except on special occasions when I'd overstepped the bounds of insider trading just the teensiest little bit or on Saturday night when she was in the most fertile part of her cycle.

I felt proud I'd supplied Joanie with a fistful of the best credit cards and it was just an idle inquiry when I noticed she was wearing a new ring. She held it out proudly. Fancy gold work, sort of a little cage with a piece of something inside that looked like Augustine. Glanced over. He was still on the window sill and I felt unworthy for my suspicions.

"What's that?"

"Oh, you have such good luck with your relic that I went on the internet and got a piece of a saint for myself. This is St. Zita. I had Tiffany's mount her for me."

"Who's St. Zita?"

"I wanted a saint especially for someone trying to get pregnant but you know how it is on the internet. You take what you can get. Zita is actually the saint of lost keys. But angels used to help her so I went for it. She sounds pretty nice and I got her cheap."

Still, nothing happened. I started to think maybe the saints, dedicated as they were to virginity, weren't possibly the best sort of help.

"Let's put the relics away for a while. Maybe they don't like what we're doing."

After all, we were pretty inventive in bed. Maybe Augustine had been a man of the world but now he lived on the kitchen windowsill, always in the kitchen like a retired old grandpa. Zita was right there on her finger all the time and she'd been one of those consecrated virgins. We put them both in her jewelry box, thinking what they didn't see wouldn't influence them and anyway we went back to pretty straightforward stuff.

Bingo! Wasn't more than a week before she didn't get her period and pretty soon it all checked out. We were certified parents-to-be. Secretly, I looked forward to bathing my baby and swishing St. Augustine through the bath water. Talk about raising a super-child. I started to investigate the entrance requirements for the best pre-schools. Harvard entrance starts when you're born.

On the other hand, I'd had a bad week at the market and we were down more money than I let on.

I proposed that I take Augustine out of the drawer but she leave Zita in there.

"I don't see why. I'm pregnant already. I don't want to make her mad. After all, even if she doesn't like sex, she probably likes babies."

She put the ring on her finger again. I figured our fertility problem had proved to be one of the temporary flukes they told us about in Wharton. I had Augustine set into an old-fashioned fob for the pocket watch I'd started to wear (with my ulcer, scotch drinking was a thing of the past and so Gus lost his swimming pool) and in due course, our daughter Ashley (of course), future member of Excelsior Nursery School and Harvard University, burst into the world.

Summer

You don't expect the sky of your life to be totally unclouded but you don't, at least in my case I didn't, expect gorgeous spring weather to be followed by a late summer of unbroken clouds, thunder, and hurricanes.

Life changed. Instead of lying naked on a down comforter in front of the fire, we took out a subscription to an experimental theater company that performed in an abattoir and invited my colleagues and clients to stuffy, boring dinners. We started paying through the nose for Ashley, three, to have twice-weekly sessions with a therapist for anxiety. I had to start watching carbs.

Other stuff happened. Not only did I have to pay a big parking fine for taking the same chances I used to get away with, they put the boot on my wheel and I was towed. One day after we'd dallied a bit in the morning and I dashed in late to work, I met my boss, who didn't say anything but looked at his watch.

It was no surprise that Mother's Day turned out to be ominous. I'd awakened that morning with butterflies in my stomach but I thought it was just because I was going to take some flowers to the cemetery in close quarters with my sisters.

My mother's ashes were in the mausoleum reserved for Catholics, in the columbarium, which is a bank of brass-and-glass doors behind which you put whatever pleasant container you have decided on for your loved one's ashes. We had chosen an antique Chinese scribe's vase, blue and white, for my mother's and it looked pretty behind the little window.

Even that had been a struggle. I chose the classy vase but Diana and Betsy wanted to use a kitschy glass container of a girl sitting with a dog, which they said had held the powder she had received as a high school graduation present. Fortunately, it didn't fit the niche so they grudgingly went with my choice.

As soon as we walked up to the columbarium, I could see something was horribly wrong. No blue and white. Something colorful, round. We got the sexton to open our niche and instead of Ma, there was one of those cylindrical snack containers. Worse still, it was full of potato chips. Barbecue flavor. My elegant life was descending into burlesque.

After the requisite horror and tears, they looked at me accusingly. I'd always been Ma's favorite and now I was the golden boy that earned more money than they had ever dreamed of. All thanks to my hard work (well, and maybe St. Augustine's help) but in their minds it was just more favoritism and I should make it up to them by being responsible for all the family problems.

I knew something was brewing that was going to cost me major time and money.

"Let's not be too hasty," I said, hoping a little humor might lighten the atmosphere. After all, what could we do about it?

"Perhaps those aren't really chips. Maybe it's some new thing they're doing to ashes, compressing them into curved, chiplike shapes. Rather elegant, actually."

"And adding the fragrance of barbecue," said Diana. She had always had a sharp tongue. Now that she was older, and I was making so much money, she always seemed to be honing it on sarcasm.

"Which she never ate."

My little sister chimed in to support Betsy as she had all her life.

"She always said barbecue gave her heartburn."

Back to Diana's sharp tongue. They were like a stand-up act.

"Maybe the crematorium gave us an unasked-for upgrade to a specially made container that says potato chips. The Andy Warhol Special."

They were joining forces and looking at me the same way they did when one of their husbands lost a job or one of their kids got suspended from school and they thought I ought to fix it.

"I can't get involved in something like this. There'd be publicity. I'd become a laughingstock on the floor."

"Obviously a subject of far greater concern than your mother's stolen remains."

I slipped the sexton fifty bucks and put the potato chip can in my trunk. Nobody spoke on the way home.

As I let them off at Diana's house, I said, "How about a discreet ad in the Times? One of those, if anybody knows the whereabouts, no questions asked, etc.?"

Faithful little sister chimed in.

"Anybody who would steal a mother's ashes isn't a reader, especially of The Times. A tabloid with bare-breasted girls would be more like it. We should sue the socks off the cemetery. They didn't keep the niche locked. Somebody with a vicious sense of humor recognized the value of the vase, dumped mother out and sold it."

I was getting irritated and careless.

"You think somebody who can't read is going to recognize an antique Chinese vase? For all they know, we might have got it at the Dollar Store."

Betsy slammed the door. They stomped off to have drinks and excoriate me.

I called after them to let me sleep on it and we'd get together for lunch, my treat—I'd take them someplace really expensive and let them figure out what mother would have wanted us to do.

I had it in mind to find a vase so identical it could pass, put some ashes from my fireplace in it and bribe the sexton to put it back. Then I would tell my sisters I'd raised hell and they'd found her in a store room. Some cock and bull story so improbable they'd accept it as true. I'd say, let's still go out for a fantastic lunch with champagne to celebrate. I know them so well. Bitchy they may be but totally bribable.

It wasn't that I didn't care my mother's ashes had probably been dumped on the way out of the cemetery and were even now blowing around Heavenly Acres. I'd loved Ma more than maybe she ever knew. I hoped she'd died knowing. She was a good woman, maybe one of the last people in the world you could say that about. She'd always helped me out of any trouble I got in as well as distributing largesse to every bum wandering the streets of New York. She'd been a sucker for every bleeding heart story in the naked city. Time after time we'd come home from school and there'd be some homeless woman there smelling the place up and waiting for dinner.

But since there wasn't a ghost of a chance of finding her real ashes, I decided I might as well cut my losses. Ma would understand like she'd always understood everything about everybody.

It wasn't actually such a bad deal to be blowing in the wind instead of stuck in a vase in a columbarium. Still, I found myself looking in the windows of every antique store and every pawnshop I passed. You don't like to think of your mother's ashes, or even her empty vase, kicking so lost around the world but what with one thing and another, I let the summer go by without doing anything about it, in spite of the weekly phone calls from big and little sister to see if I had done just that.

Fall

Autumn. You always think it's never going to happen, but, sooner or later, with maybe a little break for Indian summer, autumn always comes. We didn't have sex much anymore. Now that little Ashley was ten, Joanie had hired a Parisian au pair for child care and they spent all their time together giggling in French. She didn't seem to miss us at all.

Joanie had her activities, supposedly yoga and Pilates and art openings, all of which, strangely, seemed to happen in the evenings.

I went back to drinking, watching TV and trying to ignore the ulcer pain.

One evening, while I was sitting there ignoring the twinges in my stomach and swigging Laphroig single malt, not even bothering to give St. Augustine his share, and letting CNN tell me all the things I should be worrying about, the announcer said it was the anniversary of 9/11. It was hard to realize how much time had gone by and all of a sudden it struck me how much of my life had been tied up in ashes.

I looked at St. Augustine there dangling from my watch chain like some petrified partial Siamese twin, like something you'd see at a freak show. A chunk of rock, a cinder, a clinker I'd taken on trust all these years. First from the renegade priest who'd sold him to me and then from Joanie when she'd found him in the lining of her coat.

For more years than I liked to think about, I'd taken care of a chunk of petrifaction. A niggling little thought surfaced in whatever brain I had left after so many years of Wall Street and scotch. Had I ever taken care of anybody else that well? Might it be partly my fault that my wife was never home and my daughter preferred the babysitter?

I'd spent years of my life safeguarding a bit of cinder because I thought it was the last piece of some important person that only I had. I hated to admit it but the most important thing hadn't been that he was a saint but that I had the only known bit of him on earth. Then when the ashes of another important person in my life disappeared, all I thought about was how not to get any bad publicity, and I'd never done a damn thing about the empty niche in the columbarium.

The natural light was fading as I sat there, and I didn't bother to turn on the lights. The last of the scotch was just the warm and watery bit you get when the ice cubes have melted. I started to think about when I would turn into dust.

All of a sudden I got the proverbial flash of light and understood why the people in ancient times used ashes as a sign of mourning. It wasn't because they were the last remaining fragments of someone, with power to change your life. The power they had to change you was when you realized they were just carbon chunks, and everything was up to you. That was the part I hadn't got right.

With my sisters usually not speaking and my wife on the verge of leaving me, for sure having an affair, my daughter seeming only comfortable and happy with a paid provider, I wondered if there was time to do a Scrooge? Do a Green Acres, like that corny old TV show you see sometimes when you're channel surfing on cable, along with *Leave It to Beaver*, *Rin Tin Tin* and *Lawrence Welk*? Move out and live a simple life. Become hippies, alternative people who raised vegetables and had a little house with solar panels. Send our kid to public school, for crissake.

Realized in the next instant, there's no going back once you've worn Jimmy Choos and driven a Jag. If Scrooge had had some life style, he probably wouldn't have been so impressed with the spirits that came to visit him. Alone in that decaying mansion, it must have been easy to repent but we weren't going to leave Fifth Avenue behind.

I looked around at my lifestyle—raw silk drapes, leather furniture, real gold-leaf ceiling—which often brought comfort, but all I realized was that I was alone there in my gorgeous apartment with big windows overlooking sparkling Manhattan, my high-maintenance ten-year-old texting her friends, the stacked au pair girl making cocoa in the kitchen, and my beloved wife out looking for life where I wasn't.

So I stuck a bottle in either pocket and wandered the city, the wind blowing high up like in an H.P. Lovecraft story, a night weird things were on their way. Ended up at Ground Zero, where in spite of the park it still smelled scorched, and you wanted to hold your breath so you didn't inhale the ashes that blew around the fragile urban trees.

Over near where some contracting equipment loomed in the shadows like something out of a Stephen King horror movie, I found one of those scratched and dusty plastic chairs, those molded ones that are the most omnipresent object on earth, found on mountain tops, in deserts and jungles, indestructible, and with us until the end of time. I sat down and had another drink out of the bottle in my right pocket.

"Everything okay, bud?"

A guard looked at me suspiciously, but a five-hundred-dollar suit and the scent of really good scotch allays a lot of doubt. That plus the twenty I slipped him for being trouble.

"I had friends there."

"Yeah? We get a lot of guys like you. Three thousand people incinerated, that's quite a few friends. They're still finding bits and pieces. Rooftops, vacant lots. The ashes spread out a lot farther than you'd have thought. Nights like this, everybody seems to get lonely."

He didn't mind drinking out of the bottle so we alternated for a while. He squatted down beside me and lighted up, chain-smoked, flicking the ashes out into the darkness. Funny, with all the ashes around us, he made a few more. We're ashmakers, us humans. We've got the Midas touch of destruction, and everything we touch turns to ashes. We leave instructions to be incinerated, or someone does it for us. Eventually. All you can do is hope nobody dumps your ashes out of your fragile final home.

We talked about this and that, how the weather had changed since 9/11, sports, the price of gas.

My friend said it was time to make his rounds.

"Be careful around here. You may not credit it but there's a lot of human animals prowling this place. I always have the feeling maybe a lot of stuff's not human, too. The guards, we see and hear funny stuff. You got a home, bud? Better get on along pretty soon."

When I was alone again, I finished what was left in the bottle, took St. Augustine off the chain, and held him in my hand for a while. I'd almost lost Joanie when she'd lost Augustine, but maybe she'd been headed in the right direction.

Maybe it was time I lost St. Augustine for good. It wasn't easy, but it wasn't like I was throwing him away for nothing.

"Thanks for everything, Gus, but I'll try taking care of myself now. I think they need you here more than I do."

With that, I threw him into the darkness. I didn't want to think about what was there. Looked around. My friend the guard wasn't anywhere near. I had a feeling I should get away.

I took out my pocket handkerchief and used it to scoop up a good big handful of earth, thinking it'd still be full of ashes. Was I scooping up someone I'd spent Friday nights with? Some of the kids that were in the nursery school? Maybe some tourists that had come to line up on the mezzanine for half-price tickets to faded musicals? Maybe a bit of all of them?

I put the wad in my pocket, disregarding the acrid smell and the fact my suit would have to go to the cleaner tomorrow. I said a little prayer of thanks that I wasn't ashes there with my friends. I still had a wife and a child, and for that I was profoundly grateful. Where there's life, there's hope.

Tomorrow I'd have breakfast with Ashley, and I'd ask Joanie if she'd like to go away for a little vacation. Maybe I could be like a phoenix, that legendary bird that lives a thousand years, lays an egg and then goes up in a burst of flame, springing into life from the egg, a new bird grown out of the ashes of the old. That's one of the benefits of education. Any amount of time spent as a classics major gives you a lot of tools to describe the ups and downs of life.

I'd talk things over with Joanie and tell her what I'd done with St. Augustine. That in itself would give me points. She'd lost Zita a long time ago and gotten so she was pretty sarcastic about Gus.

Maybe she'd confess she lost Augustine after all. I'd always had a suspicion that I'd been sheltering a cuckoo all these years. If she hadn't told me yet, maybe that meant she didn't want to take away what little bit of comfort I still had, maybe that meant there was still a chance for all of us to be saved.

I'll give it a good try, anyway, after I find a blue-and-white vase to put these ashes in and give Diana and Betsy a call. Winter could still be pretty far off.

The BVM

BEFORE MOVING TO CALIFORNIA, I had never seen a Blessed Virgin Mary tree, but everything crazy starts here, folks say.

People see the BVM in lots of places all over the world but BVM trees are particularly prevalent in California. Even here, I doubt I would have seen one except for living in a trailer park.

Now I can see it's one of the blessings of living below the poverty level on nothing but Social Security.

Hunger sharpens all your senses and makes you look at things a lot more carefully.

You never hear of folks in a higher socioeconomic level seeing the BVM. I suppose they do, in fancy cathedrals or European museums, but maybe they just don't pass the word along. Keep it secret, make it sort of an "in" thing, if you know what I mean, like not wearing polyester and drinking micro-brewery beer.

They wouldn't have to see her in a tree or a sandwich or a paint spill like we do. I expect they would see her in the folds of a silk ball gown or in the rocks they get for their scotch whiskey out of sub-zero iceboxes, but who am I to say they don't see her for their needs as much as we do for ours.

I'm not such a fool as to think money always brings happiness nor that poverty is enriching. I'm only telling you that you can have some happiness without money.

Here in the trailer park, we're matier, tell one another, put notices of sightings on the bulletin board in the laundry room, invite people to come over, have a cup of coffee, and look at wherever she's revealed herself to us.

Not just trees, either. We see her everywhere. I tend to notice the trees more since I wasn't brought up here. They're a California tradition, and I'm from Pennsylvania.

Most have the wrong idea about trailer dwellers. We're not just folks who sit in front of the tube, and when we do, we watch the news or documentaries as often as *Jeopardy* or sitcoms. We may be undereducated but we're not stupid. I'm not saying we don't keep up on Jerry Springer but we know the difference between the BVM and something that just looks like her.

You may ask how we know the difference. Well, that's hard to explain. Just a sort of feeling in our hearts like when you walk over to the phone before it rings, and it's your sister you haven't heard from for ten years.

Sometimes an oil slick in the street is just a pretty oil slick, and sometimes it's like a stained-glass window you can look through into heaven.

At any rate, we don't swallow sightings hook, line, and sinker the way the TV crews make out we do when they choose those of us with the worst grammar to interview on TV.

Mary Suarez gets a kick out of those crews and makes sure she talks to them soon as they arrive, fills her sentences with what she calls double negatives and unlawful use of "them" as a demonstrative adjective, and I don't know what-all.

She laughs when she tells us what she does, but it doesn't make a whole lot of sense to me. She's got a Ph.D. but she's fallen. I just finished high school, but I speak pretty well, neither too bad nor too fancy. Just ordinary.

Before the BVM came to the tree stump, I'd only heard about her being in a lot of other places—steamy windows, grilled cheese sandwiches, billboards on the highway overpass, oil spills on the roads, but never in something permanent like a tree.

That may be because in my walk of life most things are transient and undependable, and I never did get out into nature much. When I think about it, I can see how it would have seemed more likely I'd see the BVM in some melted ice cream in the cut-rate supermarket, but after the tree sighting, I'd join my neighbors in pooling gas money, make a sandwich and have a pleasurable outing to look at the stump, spend the evening in the light of the votive candles people set around, talk a little, sing a hymn, all in the cool, fresh cemetery air.

Our park's a couple of miles outside Colma, just south of San Francisco, that in 1924 incorporated as a necropolis and took in all the dead San Francisco was evicting from the holes where they'd hoped to wait for Jesus, or maybe Moses in the case of the Jewish part, or Muhammed. I guess non-believers were just expecting to rot.

It's a little place, Colma. Well, they say the population's two million, but that's a joke. That's only if you add up all the cemeteries here, sixteen of them. Colma's got about eleven hundred alive, not counting the trailer parks. We're the no-'count folks, we say. Not counted in any official count, see? Trailer people have a sense of humor, if nothing else.

We've also got eight tombstone carvers, ten florists, a historic Irish pub, and twelve car dealers, don't ask me why. A lot of famous and semi-famous people are buried here, including Wyatt Earp, who's buried in Eternity, the Jewish section, although he wasn't Jewish, Joe DiMaggio, Levi Strauss of blue jean fame, and Tina Turner's beloved dog, wrapped in Tina's mink coat.

My boy who works in the body shop, when I told him about the BVM in the tree stump, said, "Oh yeah, I see those alla time, the BVM in dents on wrecked cars, usually ones where someone got killed."

He was joking but I brought him up better than that, had him baptized and confirmed. I said to him, "Isn't that what you would expect of the BVM, to bring consolation to the dying?"

He just looked sceptical and remoted to another channel. He likes to sit in company while he watches TV, but he doesn't talk a whole lot.

I wondered if she appeared to them as a comfort. That would mean a dent on the inside of the car and my boy was talking about dents on the outside. He was cracking his third brew and I didn't think I wanted to get him started. He's a good boy but rough around the edges from his line of work.

"Grandma," my five-year-old, his little boy, said, "Look at my quarter. There's a pretty lady on it. That's the BVM, isn't it?"

My boy's wife Aileen said I was filling him up with a lotta nonsense and maybe I should stop sitting him. She's Pentecostal and after six years of marriage to my boy still suspicious of Catholics, especially after a hard day of work in the Buick dealership where she keeps the cars shined up, but I defend my only grand to everyone.

"If he says it's the BVM, then it is. Blessed are the pure in heart, and you're certainly pure, aren't you, darling?"

However, I made sure I took Aileen an extra big helping of Snickers Salad, made with plenty of Cool Whip and sugar, with Snickers bars chopped up in it, out of the *White Trash Cookbook*. For the rich who are into gourmet, it's a joke, but it's full of the recipes I grew up with and a lot of good down-home cooking and easily accessible ingredients, too.

"What are you talking about? You're not too big to enjoy a bite of dessert," I said.

She patted my hand, and I knew I'd been forgiven, but my boy glared at me because he's said more than once, and even in front of her, that he's not going to the tavern on Friday night with anyone wearing a size 22. Still, she's got creamy skin and a pretty face so I think he might be content with that.

Later I whispered to little Tukey, my grandson, that the BVM was our secret and he shouldn't talk about it to his mom. I said we'd have cookies and talk about her if he kept it a secret. My heart would break if she took that sweet little boy away from me one day before he has to start school and get all rough the way they do.

For five, he's a deep thinker. A while back, after he heard something on TV, he said to me, "Grandma, is it really the BVM in the cheese sandwich or is it just a picture of her?"

I said it was a mystery, and we mortals couldn't know, but we should be respectful just in case. It was then he got so slow in his eating because he examines every little bite to make sure he isn't chomping down on the BVM.

"Nope," I'll hear him say, and then he'll start to chew.

Bless his heart, when I took him to the mall to see Santa last week, he said, "Grandma, I bet if we bought a cinnamon bun, if the BVM would be there in it, we could save it and sell it to get a new trailer, but if she's not there, we could eat it."

At $3.95 a bun, I couldn't get one for him, but when we got home, I made him some pancakes and put lots of brown sugar on top since we were out of syrup.

Anyway, it was after that item on the news about the BVM in the cemetery that the furor started. It'd gotten to where quite a few of the faithful came on nice evenings and weekends to spend a few hours with her.

After that news story, I stopped going for a while because I didn't like to fight through the crowds, figured I'd just wait until they all rushed off to see something new, like the BVM on top of Golden Gate Bridge or something, and then we could go back to taking our lawn chairs over and enjoying the evening air. In the meantime, I could see the BVM in plenty of other places.

But when I saw on the news where the church dignitaries were going to go see the stump, I thought I'd mosey over and see what was going on.

There's not that much excitement around here, and I didn't want to miss seeing an Archbishop. I could see that it would be an important marker in future times, "the year before I saw the Archbishop" or "three years after the Archbishop came to see the BVM in the cemetery tree stump." I didn't want to feel left out in years to come.

I thought I'd get there early, but by the time I arrived, they'd already marked off the area around the tree and a path out to the road with that bright orange incident tape like they use on television. There were half a dozen police cars there and swirling lights and walkie-talkies going on, and I debated just going home, but I'd brought my lawn chair, so I thought I might as well stay, and I was glad I did. I can remember it as plain as if it were yesterday, and what I didn't notice, somebody else did.

We've retold this story hundreds of times now, and we've helped one another remember all the little details that just slipped by unnoticed at the time, so you can be sure this is the total picture.

Quantities of black cars pulled in sort of all of a sudden, and the place was filled with men in the most gorgeous robes imaginable, and the police lights went around like I remember the strobe light rotating on the ceiling of the school gym at my prom, illuminating all us girls in our fluffy dresses except this time it was the vestments, and let me tell you, those nuns that dress their men can *embroider*! Silver, gold, all the colors of the rainbow, you've never seen the like!

After milling around a bit, the clerical group formed themselves into a procession about a hundred yards from the stump and stepped off in a very dignified manner.

We were all behind the police tape watching them move in like it was the Academy Awards, but instead of waving and shouting most of us knew enough to genuflect and cross ourselves, so we wouldn't have anything of disrespect we'd have to confess later.

I tell you, we've remembered that procession dozens of times and each time, as we add details, it seems finer.

In front of the procession came half a dozen pretty boys in black and white lace-trimmed robes bearing lighted candles, followed by a priest swinging incense in a heavy brass burner on a long chain like in church but swinging it in the fanciest pattern I'd ever seen, over and around in complete circles, in figure eights, as showy as a majorette marching down the street in the Parade of Roses. Everybody before and behind gave him plenty of room, you can be sure of that. The clouds of incense drifted around the cemetery like the smudge pots they put in the orange groves when a rare freeze is expected.

Then the cross held on high came, preceded by a little girl in a white first-communion dress, the only female in the procession, skipping ahead and scattering rose petals out of a basket.

Then came four priests carrying a fancy four-cornered four-posted canopy over another priest bearing a monstrance like a burnished gold sun with the Host inside. I guess they thought He'd recognize his mother and give them some kind of sign they could believe, sort of like Mexican jumping beans when you hold them in your palm and they start to bump and wriggle.

After all that, on his snow-white horse, came the Archbishop himself, made even taller by his grand gold-embroidered mitre. Walking beside him was a boy carrying a silken cushion, on it a monkey dressed up in a red velvet suit with a little tasseled gold cap on its head, sitting up nibbling on a cookie as nice and polite as anything you'd ever seen.

Following at a respectful distance came several lesser bishops in plain white satin mitres, all gorgeously robed in lace and purple and green and gold, mounted on prancing steeds, attended by pages with tassels on their shoes, thin little greyhounds with bells on their collars running along beside them.

Oh, they were a lovely sight moving through the wood, with the robed choir chanting, the flickering candles illuminating all the gold, banners waving, and the smell of incense mixing with the fragrance of pine trees.

I tell you, it wasn't the sort of company you take for granted in a trailer park, and we savored every detail.

We talked about it for years, everybody adding details they had noticed that had escaped other people until we had a good picture in our mind's eye, and for the rest of our days, when we remembered that evening, people would still be adding some grand detail they hadn't remembered before.

Old Mrs. Zervas told us several years afterward that what she remembered best was the elephant. A white one, she said, looming out of the mist, with a blue tapestry hanging down its sides, and a little gold house on its back, to carry the BVM's tree stump away, she figured.

That was what she said she remembered, but she'd been waiting several years to get her cataracts operated on, so I don't know how much of that is true. All I can say is no one else remembered an elephant. I could see she felt we were holding back a little, and she said kind of defiantly that it was waiting under the trees, in the shadows.

Who's to say what a body sees or doesn't see?

Betty from the double wide two rows over said that after Mrs. Zervas passed, we wouldn't have to remember that part any more, but I said IMHO she didn't have anything else to leave anybody and it would be an act of kindness to continue remembering the elephant. Maybe even add a little boy with a turban and a jeweled stick sitting behind its head, and the one time it lifted its trunk and trumpeted, probably when the BVM was on the move, kind of like when they ring the little bell up on the altar.

I don't mind telling you I was close enough to see some details I remembered long after the stump had been taken away, like the broken, tied shoelace the Archbishop was wearing and the blob of mustard near a Bishop's mouth, left over from his lunch, I expect. Maybe not the prettiest details but the good and the bad together make up the whole truth, I always say.

Not one of them in the procession looked like the kind of person you'd ask into your trailer for a piece of cake and a cup of coffee, but we have to hope they were experts at what they were doing. Probably being professional debunkers is a wearing profession, and they'd lived with too much disappointment.

They marched in procession to the stump. The Archbishop scowled at it for about thirty seconds, then turned away, and started to stomp back to the cars. After him, the Bishops looked at it, turned their noses up, and did the same. The others didn't even bother to look, and their procession back wasn't nearly as stately as their arrival. They blew the candles out and the incense burner hung on its chain with no fragrance at all drifting out.

By the time they were all getting back in the cars and loading the horses in trailers, the bulldozer swooped out of someplace we hadn't noticed, and before we knew what was happening, it scooped the stump out of the ground and put it in the black pickup that followed the Archbishop's cars away, taking it to the Vatican, I presume, where it's probably stored in the Pope's basement to this day.

After they left, we just milled around the hole where they'd pulled up the stump, sort of disconsolate and lonely, like after your daughter's wedding when she and her new husband have pulled out for their honeymoon, and you're left to clear up all the platters.

It was my friend Vera who called us all to come over to where she'd walked up to another tree, a nice young growing oak this time instead of a chopped off maple stump like the one they'd hauled away, and right there, clear as the photo of my sainted mother that sits on top of my television, was a picture of not only the BVM but the Holy Child as well, formed out of bark growing in a complicated pattern, with some tree sap forming her glowing golden-brown hair.

She hadn't gone away with them at all, just transferred herself to a new and even better dwelling place.

"All they've got in that pickup to store away in the darkness is a stump of wood," I said, and we looked at each other and smiled, the kind of smile you smile when you've thought of just the right answer to the snippy clerk in the welfare office, but when we tacked a notice on the laundry room bulletin board with a little map I drew on the back of the electric company bill, I wrote, "Let's keep it quiet this time, folks," and so far as I know, everybody's kept quiet because we're still carrying our lawn chairs out there to enjoy the BVM and take the evening air, and she's stopped one toothache, eased everybody's arthritis, and cured Perry Idolia of his occult cancer.

We're back to normal now. The BVM shows up all over the place, sort of like Elvis. The trees are still special, but people see her in the unlikeliest places and as usual, tack up a notice in the laundry room for the trailer park community. We don't always go to look if we're feeling poorly because we know she'll pop up right in front of us sooner or later.

See, when you live with her, it's not like taking her for granted, but like thinking of her as a daughter. Even if you don't see her for a while, she'll always show up again, and you'll smile at her, offer her a piece of fresh-baked pie, and you'll both pick up where you left off, talking a mile a minute.

There are slow weeks when nobody finds a new tree or sandwich and when even the oil slicks (that are usually totally dependable) seem like nothing but . . . oil slicks. At times like that, we just keep our eyes open.

A lot of times you see her up in a cloud. That's a pretty reliable sighting place. You carry your folding chair out in front of your trailer, where you've got morning glory vines trained up strings to your windows, and there she is, up in heaven, great piles of creamy robes in the middle of a celestial California blue sky, and you think she'll stay a while, so you go inside for a minute to refill your cup of coffee.

But what with wind moving aloft even if the trees are still, she's like your daughter when she's curled up on the sofa daydreaming of love. You know she's gonna jump up and be off when the phone rings. That BVM cloud may seem steady, but stormy winds will often be moving in from somewhere on earth, like the troubles you know are waiting for your daughter, who's three months gone but hasn't told you yet.

She won't stay there in the clouds for long, Our Lady, or in the sandwich, or in the pattern of leaves on the sidewalk after a rain storm, or even in a sturdy tree stump in a cemetery, so you just have to love her while you can, knowing she's like the proverbial bad penny that always turns up again or that good luck two-dollar bill somebody gave you, that you sometimes find tucked in a book where you used it to mark your place and sometimes crumpled in with the laundry, so you just take it out of the dryer, shove it in your apron pocket, and then forget it until you find it again.

From time to time, someplace or other, often where and when you expect her least, she'll show up.

Might be in something holy where you'd expect to find her, like the swirls of incense in church, but more likely in the soap-suds as you scrub your kitchen floor.

I can tell you, she's got a sense of humor because, one day last week, I was looking in the mirror to comb out the new perm Perry Idolia's daughter-in-law gave me, and there she was in the wrinkles in my face.

I had a real good time with that one, walking up to everyone I met and saying, "Look at my face. Do you see the Virgin?"

Almost everybody did, at least saying, "Yeah, there's something around your eyes or your chin or your hairline," like you do when somebody shows you a baby and asks does it look like their side of the family.

Listen, don't try to find her. That's the worst possible thing you can do. Just go on doing all the stuff you have to do to get through life and forget about her, and then, when you least expect it, the BVM, she'll show up and give you the surprise of your life. Oil spills, sandwiches, wrinkles. . . .

Like I said, she's got a sense of humor.

Sleepers Awake

I WAS HAPPY ENOUGH being a "sleeper," waiting for Armageddon, living a comfy upper-middle-class lifestyle with a hundred-dollar coffee machine and a subscription to a trendy little theatre that performed in the back alleys of Manhattan. My only obligation was easy, to lead a seemingly normal life by cohabiting with a young mortal and know I had to stay undercover until the end times came, and Satan would call me forth to help with the clean-up operation.

The daughters of humans love us demons who, because we are funded, easily outdo young men who have to work for a living. How can they compete? We are available to cook exquisite gourmet breakfasts, skilled at home-made haute-couture, adept at writing love poems, and supply massage with fingers that never tire.

The young women, for their part, bank on the end not coming during their lifetimes and find it pleasant to have partners who can shape-shift so easily, giving them variety without the necessity of hooking up in noisy clubs or even going through unpleasant serial divorces.

There is a demon for every taste. Middle-aged balding schlubs for skinny young museum administrators with horn-rimmed glasses and degrees in art history, ripped demons who look great in spandex for roller derby professionals, foodies whose scorching breath caramelizes the best crème brûlées ever, with never a need for the kitchen's handy little propane blowtorch, and demons of endlessly inventive prowess in the dark for enchanted nymphomaniacs.

Finding young women isn't a problem nor is it true we are averse to white weddings in strait-laced Anglican churches. We view ourselves as cultural anthropologists and take an interest in all earthly customs. We bond with wedding planners and revel in details of bridal showers. Our bachelor parties are as legendary back home in Hell as on earth. After we are wed, we flirt with the vicar regardless of gender and swing the thurible in robed processions, stir up good-natured trouble while sitting on the vestry, and take on Sunday School classes, where we help five-year-olds make clay models of the crucifixion.

My tale of woe began with the Upper West Side coven, a typical small demon-human community that enjoys retro parties with brittle conversation and 40's cocktails, where house keys are thrown into the middle of the floor, and all go home with partners of fortune. It was not well received, therefore, when, like a lightning bolt from Heaven (alas, yes), true love burst forth from me and my partner one Lammas Eve, that holiday of ripeness, late summer warmth and fruitfulness promising provocatively the joys of Halloween and winter.

We'd been together for five years and were starting to take each other for granted when for some reason, who knows, perhaps a little joke from Cupid, at that fatal party, our eyes met and sparks flew. All thoughts of other partners for that night flew away like bats out of Hell.

Ignoring quizzical glances, we slammed out the door, dived into my new BMW Z4 Roadster, and raced home, babbling of passion all the way to bed, only stopping at an all-night convenience store long enough to buy a bouquet of flowers and an assortment of sugar-dripping doughnuts for our next morning's agape feast, thinking the occasion demanded relaxation from a healthful flaxseed cereal breakfast.

Then the first night of true love I have ever known ensued. I pulled out some little tricks I had never used. Smoky fifteen-year-old GlenDronach single malt (hints of sherry and not too fruity) mixed with water for passion, from Ammon's stream that boils hot in the chilly morning and icy cold at midday, water that will set wood on fire under the full moon.

In the Jacuzzi, water from the Aethipian Lake for deep, dream-filled lethargies, a touch of the heavy water of the Ciccones for a touch of madness, a jolt of clear water from the Sybaris to shift the molecules of her already honey-drenched hair to the brightness of clover and wildflowers. Sated, we slept together in a night of miracles and whispers.

For the first time, no shape shifting wanted. Nothing but her beloved body for me and, I think I can truthfully say, my beloved body for her. From that night on, we walked hand-in-hand. She quit her no-longer-needed ego-supporting work as the assistant to a much-whispered-about *Vogue* photographer, possible successor to Annie Leibovitz. We spent our days together twenty-four-seven, discussed having a baby, and decided we couldn't take so much time away from each other.

Of course, our young married crowd found such fidelity boring. We were no longer invited to parties but so absorbed were we in love we airily dismissed the scorn in former friends' eyes and voices when we happened to meet. We were a couple, a Pyramis and Thisbe, a Darby and Joan, planning to spend our eternities hand-in-hand, and so it is sad we were together (of course) in the World Trade Center when it blew, in the vestibule getting half-price tickets to see our favorite, *A Chorus Line*, for the forty-fifth time.

Thinking the Last Days had come, I used my silk Sulka necktie to tie our wrists together, as I had seen a couple do in a shipwreck scenario on a late-night show and with a gel pen inscribed a protective 666 on her forehead, planning to buy enough time to enroll her in a demonic witness protection program that would let our love continue, but the destruction was complete beyond Sodom and Gomorrah, beyond the flood, beyond the expulsion from Heaven, and she turned to ashes in my arms while I survived, of course, unscorched.

The coven waited for me to recover, set me up with luscious screenwriters, lissome massage therapists, even, thinking I might be in a serious mood, a music librarian from the Pratt Institute.

All to no avail and eventually, finding me almost a suburban bore, left me alone to my own devices, saying only, when we met in coffee shops or the liquor store, *hey, good to see you, let's get together one of these days*, and we all knew what that meant.

It's okay. I don't want to see them, fools who have never known love. Now, unshaven, in dirty old bespoke shirts and un-pressed Armani suits, I leave the answering machine turned off and no longer carry a cell phone. I sit with dictionary and the-saurus, write love poems all day, and read them at open mikes in the evening. Then, sipping nostalgic GlenDronach from a brown paper bag, I ride the subway to the site of her funeral pyre with the days' poems, touch them with the flame from my two-thousand-dollar Caran d'Ache Écaille lighter (from the days I cared about such things), throw their ashes into the wind-tossing air eddies at Ground Zero, and wait, with faith, for the time we'll surely be together again, at Armageddon.

Godly Gadgets

THE FIRST SIGN I received that day was on the way to see my mother, always a little stress-making to begin with. I ran into a woman's problem. I call it that because it's probably not a problem for most of you guys, but it's something a lot of us women can relate to.

You're walking down the street minding your own business. You're deep in thought and don't even notice the vague figure of a man leaning up against a building until he says something to you.

"What?" you say, coming to a stop and looking at this complete stranger in a puzzled way. Then he says it again.

"Hey, little lady, howja like to give me a blow job?"

Well, believe me, nothing you learn from Miss Manners prepares you for this situation. All your mother ever said was to ignore people who said rude things. Am I right?

At first I thought of just touching my rubber holy medal, one of my own products, and saying to him the little prayer that comes with it,

"I'm rubber and you're glue. Whatever you say bounces off me and sticks to you."

But that's too easy. You don't want to just walk away, because THIS GUY NEEDS TO BE PUNISHED! You want him to suffer, at least a little.

Well, here's the skinny I've figured out. There's usually an audience. He's got his buddies leaning on the wall with him, waiting to see the fun.

If you've got the nerve, you can look at his zipper and say, "Well, haul it out and let me take a look before I make a decision."

This is one where you can't lose. Chances are he's not going to do it.

Then you can say, "If people don't let me inspect the merchandise, I figure there's something wrong with it."

If he does have the nerve to unzip and haul it out (and with buddies there to egg him on, he very well might), you can give it a considering look and show disappointment, maybe even shake your head a little. No matter what size or shape it is, you can show disappointment.

It's even better if you're with a girlfriend. You can look at each other and shake your heads with a pitying look. Then you smile kindly, say, "I don't think so," and walk away. See what I mean. He can't win and you can't lose.

Oh, walk away fast. You may be in danger.

I couldn't believe it. The day hardly started and already two major bad signs. The first? Oh, that was before I'd even left home. I wish I'd taken it as a sign I should stay home and get back in bed.

Just as I was tearing out the door, the phone rang, so I went back in and answered. So far as signs go, that's a tough one—the phone ringing just as you go out the door but before you've managed to close it. It can mean fate is giving you a chance for happiness if you're quick enough to dash back and hear you've won a prize or something, or it can be fate getting ready to lay some heavy trip on you that you can miss if you're a little slower. I'm so incurably hopeful I always try to get back in time to answer.

Anyway, it was someone from a . . . utility . . . company. Yes, I had neglected to pay my . . . utility . . . bill. This doesn't make me a bad woman. I've been stressed out lately. I'm not saying I was right. I was wrong. It keeps the world going to pay bills on time. I think. It's somewhere in there with ethics, morality, and cleanliness (the one that's next to godliness).

Anyway, I dropped everything and tore back in the house to answer the phone. No name. That whispery voice anonymous callers usually use when they call at two in the morning.

"You've got three business days to pay or we're going to turn your . . . utility . . . off."

Now let's face it. He's not gonna get paid much, not for a job like calling people to deliver nasty messages, and so you wouldn't think he could identify so much with his employers.

You'd think he would have worded his message a little bit sympathetically, something more like, "I can't believe I have to do this in order to put groceries on my table, but believe it or not, I have to tell you that the money-grubbing bloodsuckers I work for, who unfortunately have a monopoly on supplying you with this precious stuff you must have in order to live, are going to turn off your . . . utility . . . and not give you a second thought if you don't cough up in three business days."

I could have lived with that.

What I couldn't bear were the sly insinuations in his voice. What was unsaid was this:

Yeah, I hear you there stuttering and promising. We both know you're not going to make it. You couldn't mail the check in on time, and you probably don't have enough in your account anyway. You're just not that kind of person.

Furthermore, your roof is probably leaking and you have rats in your foundation. Your son is going to end up in prison on grand theft auto, and your daughter is going to have seventeen children with no husband. Oh, yeah, your husband, if you ever manage to get one, will cheat on you, too.

You have a horrible incurable disease percolating away somewhere in your innards, and it will be inoperable by the time it's discovered. I wouldn't worry about it too much, not with the life you have.

Everything you ever attempt is going to come to nothing. What's left of your life is going to be dismal and discouraging. You're not ever going to lose that ten pounds you've been carrying around, and you just might take up smoking in the near future hoping for some foolish misjudged comfort.

Oh, by the way, this might be a good time to let you know you didn't win the Publishers Sweepstakes either.

Have a nice day.

Yeah, it got me down for a while, but I'm not ashamed of being a late payer. This is one small gesture I can make to say "Maybe I can't wear midriff-baring fashions, and maybe my protest sign is gathering dust in the basement, but I can still live close to the edge, and by God, I'm going to pay you late the next time, too!"

However, on this particular day I'm talking about, it was my mother's birthday, so after these two unsettling episodes, I shook off my feelings of foreboding and continued on my way to Ma's house to celebrate with a nicely gift-wrapped Day of Judgment coffee mug from my business stock—about which more later—and a tutti-frutti fudge cake, her favorite.

With this beginning I wasn't too much of a happy camper on my way. To make it worse, I knew I was gonna end up discussing (1) when was I going to settle down religion-wise and become something she could tell her friends about, (2) why didn't I get married so she could tell her friends about it, and (3) why was I in such a weird business she couldn't even tell her friends about it.

Right on the nose. She started off on my religious quest before she'd even cut the cake, using that fake sweet voice of hers to put me off guard, like I'd fall for that after twenty-seven years of survival.

"Sweetheart, I know you're on a quest for a religion you can sincerely commit to but how can you go to the Episcopal Church and take communion and everything and keep right on going down to that Buddhist *zendo* and sitting *zazen*?"

I said to her, "Ma, it's just like having a nice solid marriage and a husband you're happy with, but you still keep a little something exotic on the side."

That's language my mother understands. The little something exotic on the side. I'm cool with it. Who am I to censor something that's kept my parents married for thirty-seven years? Dad has his power tools, Ma has the little something exotic on the side, and never the twain shall meet.

Actually, as long as I was just Episcopalian and Buddhist, I was calling myself an Episco-bud but now that I've started to study Islam as well, I may have to change that to being an Episco-bud-lamite. I figure if I'm ever in the hospital, I'll get plenty of clergy visitors. I'll just have to make sure the priest, the roshi and the imam don't all come on the same day.

Ma, on the other hand, is talking a lot about why I should at least go out with her girlfriend's son, one of her home boys, even if I never knew she had any religion except the International Brotherhood of Electrical Workers until I was old enough to get married. I'll be the first to admit, there's a lot to be said for Jewish guys. Those cute little caps, for one thing. Then they have the reputation for being solid husband material. Not heavy drinkers and usually hairy-chested, a little embellishment I can always relate to.

Come to think of it, I might have to fit the rabbi in on days the others don't come. Then what am I going to call myself? Judeo-episco-bud-lamite? I think maybe it's too long to fit in when you have to fill out forms, you know?

Ma made a fresh pot of tea, and once we finished with my love life, it was time to talk about my employment status. So far as jobs go, there aren't many people who can have a job working at what they truly love, so I'm grateful for every minute of the time I spend at mine. At only twenty-seven, I'm an entrepreneur with my own internet site. Godly Gadgets. That's what I call my online mini-mall. When I get a little more capital, I'm going to have my own catalog, maybe do something with QVC, even get a spot with Dr. Oz for some of my spiritual wellness products.

Ma said I ought to get a regular job and just distribute all my Godly Gadgets to the poor and the homeless. She said, in tones of foreboding and worry, "Darling, I've got very bad vibes about you making money by selling religious stuff."

I told her, "Pat Robertson and Jerry Falwell ain't doing so bad. Lookit what they say, and they haven't been struck dead. Yet. *And* they have vacation homes and drive nice cars. *And* they don't buy their clothes at K-Mart."

She should have seen me spending all day yesterday filling a rush order for Prayer Toasters and Twelve Apostles Beer Steins.

The Prayer Toaster comes with a loaf of plastic bread slices. They've each got a prayer on them. You load the toaster with bread slices once a week. Every morning you push the button and a new plastic slice of bread with a prayer pops up. You get six blank plastic slices of bread you can write your own prayers on with erasable markers. Prayers for your kids' geometry test, for example, or that your period comes on.

The Twelve Apostles Beer Stein shows the apostles in their complete robes when it's empty, but when you fill it up with beer, they don't have anything on. You might think that's sort of pornographic and sacrilegious all packed up in one, but it's symbolic or something like that. I'm not up on all the theology.

Stuff I stock? Well, there's the Holy Trinity jack-in-the-box for toddlers, where the Holy Spirit really is one, sort of like Casper the Friendly Ghost. This comes in both the Republican and Democrat model for the Big Guy and the Kid, with Sarah Palin and Rand Paul for the Republicans and Hillary and the Jolly Green Giant for the Democrats.

If you've got the big bucks (I haven't sold one of these yet), there's the hot air balloon Jesus, 110 feet tall, with hands 30 feet long. Two-hundred-eighty-five-thousand cubic feet of air! In this day and age, a nice item to float over public buildings like the Pentagon although I guess to be politically correct, maybe we'd better find a hot air Moses, a Muhammed and, so far as that goes, maybe a hot air Buddha. Maybe just a nice bland hot air God who would do for any denomination.

My own idea, the Jesus Christ phone card, has a laser logo of Jesus on it. You think of religion every time you make a call, and it's refillable with a major credit card.

Of course we sell all the usual stuff that any religious entrepreneur has—Holy Dove panty hose, a What Would Jesus Do purse container for your birth control pills (for those who are conscientious about the world population problem), the Grab a Towel When the Rapture Comes bumper sticker, the Save Your Marriage with St. Paul's Advice sweatshirt, etc.

Believe it or not, my biggest seller so far has been the St. Francis pet baptizing kit. We are truly a nation that loves animals. If you've got a stuffy priest who won't baptize turtles, you just do it yourself. We've got authentic holy water (I have an internet priest that blesses it for me over the phone), a baptismal certificate, and instructions for a lovely ceremony. Ecologically sound party favors for the after-ceremony celebration are included.

For those of you who spend more time than you feel you should in the kitchen, there's the Virgin Mary refrigerator magnet kit. Changeable outfits for everything from an awe-inspiring Theotokos, the Mother of God, to a young mom with the holy child in a stroller. It's a great gift for a new neighbor along with a plate of brownies. You might just want to check out their religious preference first. We've got plenty of other gifts if they've made a different denominational choice.

On the devotional side, I also sell a service—messages taken to your loved ones who have passed on. They're memorized by terminally ill persons who do this for their ministry. No guarantee but they'll do their best. It's a nice alternative to flowers or a charity.

Before you even ask, of course I stock the Mel Gibson Crucifixion Nail Necklace although by the time we pay Mel his cut, we're barely making cost. Still, you want your clientele to think you're on the cutting edge.

Anyway, back to the conversation with Ma. It wasn't enough she was criticizing my whole way of life. I'd bought a gorgeous cake to show her I loved her, and I thought it was a nice gesture to join her in a piece. As someone usually on a diet, was I just let to enjoy that in a quiet way? Oh, no. She made that into a problem, too. That nice sweet voice again, the one she uses when she wants to try to CONTROL MY LIFE.

"Doll, I thought you were trying to lose a couple of pounds. You're not going to eat that huge piece of cake, are you? At least scrape off the icing. Here, put it on my plate."

Oh, so casual but I knew what was going on. Once that chocolate fudge icing was on her plate, as she talked, she would absent-mindedly (ha!) pick at it until the whole pile was gone, and she could casually cut herself a whole other piece of cake. I love my ma, but I've studied her like a book, so as to eradicate undesirable inherited qualities in me, and I'd seen that little trick before.

On the day in question, since it was a special occasion, I was going to give myself a little break from my usual diet technique, and I was looking forward to a piece of that cake. Sure I'm on a diet. But I eat—chocolate, French Fries, cheesecake.

Well, maybe I should explain that a little, since we're being totally honest here. Eat . . . isn't . . . really . . . what I do. Every molecule in my body is shrieking to be rounded and buxom. I constantly have to say "Down, Fido" to my appetite. I'm familiar with different diet techniques, and, for me, something like anorexia is a distant dream, like being a rock star . . . and I can't seem to do the bulimia thing, either. When that food is in my stomach, it means to stay there. So, what I do is bite . . . and chew a while . . . then spit it out. Sort of a *coitus interruptus* of the mouth. If I don't make it with Godly Gadgets, I have it in the back of my mind to become a diet guru.

Anyway, just to make a point, I ignored my usual birth control, excuse me, I mean diet control, method and settled down calmly (on the outside, at least) to enjoy my super-large slice of cake, thinking she'd drop the whole subject when she saw she had no hope of controlling me.

Sure enough, after she'd harangued me a while about the necessity for a well-balanced diet, she started in on when was I going to get a real job. To her that means going to an office and a 401(k).

"Mom," I said, "that means interviews. You really want me to do something like that?"

"What's wrong with an interview," she asked. "Are you too good to go out and ask for a decent job after being an online CEO?"

My own mother sending me out on interviews. Can you imagine? Well, think about it. You go there dressed in clothes you hope will entice your interviewer into . . . giving you some money. You watch your posture and hold your body in a way that you hope will send a message that you deserve . . . some money. You coo in awe at the interviewer's words and say ad-

miring things, again in hope of some . . . money. Are you starting to get the picture? Let's face it: interviews are the corporate
equivalent of lap dancing.

Supposing you get this job, what then? I've tried working in
offices. They give you a silicone spray for your fingertips, so you
can scoot around the keyboard faster. I discovered I could get
the same effect dipping into a bag of potato chips. When I was
office temping, I gained twenty pounds.

Talking with ma was starting to get me down. I made my
escape move.

"Ma, I've got to get up early tomorrow for the K-Mart sale," I
said and got out the door.

On my way home from Ma and several slices of fudge cake,
I was filled with confusion as well as carbs and calories. Maybe
I was on a sugar high. I just didn't know. Maybe she was right.

See, I've spent a lot of my life looking for signs. I've turned
down marriage proposals after reading my fortune cookie. I
make my cup of yoga tea every night and lay out the paper slip
at the top of the tea bag because each one has a *penetrating* bit of
advice to guide the next day (and I don't like to eat so many fortune cookies on my diet, even if I spit them out).

Why would my life be so full of negativism if I was headed
in the right direction? If I settled down and got married, at least
I'd have a husband walking by my side when I went past creeps
on the street. I'd pay my bills on time. I wouldn't have to consider doing a lap dance so I would be allowed to speed type in
a high rise. Maybe Godly Gadgets *was* a sort of irreverent business, and God was sending me all these bad signs as warnings.

One thing I did know. There wasn't anything in my apartment for breakfast, so I stopped at the supermarket to pick up
some soy milk and low-carb tortillas and a new box of Yoga
Tea, the one with the advice on the bag tags.

I didn't know the supermarket was into signs until I looked
at my receipt as ma had taught me, to see if they'd credited me
for the buy one–get one free offers. There it was, just what I
needed to round off my life after my stressful afternoon. More

weird signs and this one was a lollapalooza, printed right on my supermarket receipt.

Right there under the figure that showed how much I had saved was this: *Everything is guaranteed.*

This was printed; this was official. I started to feel really creepy and the hair stood up on the back of my neck as the thought came to me that maybe someone unseen really is checking all of us out, all the time, sending us any signs that tickle his or her fancy.

Then I thought, maybe different people get different wishes. Get stuffed, for example. Or support your local law enforcement officer. Even, if you look hopelessly blah, have a nice day.

But who's deciding? That's what I want to know. Is someone making sure there's a creep standing in my way to make rude remarks when I'm on the way to see my mother? If so, will my rubber medal of Our Lady of the Trampoline be enough to protect me? What's the meaning I'm supposed to get out of this? Why is someone sniggering rudely at me because I'm a little late sending in the check for my . . . utility? When I'm in line at the checkout counter, who's deciding whether I should receive an encouraging message or a solicitation to donate my organs?

I grabbed my stuff and walked fast all the way home. At least weirdo wasn't propping up his wall anymore. My untidy apartment with wall-to-wall packing materials for Godly Gadgets had never looked so good.

Are you expecting some great big revelation from all this? Forget it. What my signs had taught me about life that day was just about what I'd learned every other day of my life. Whattaya gonna do except hang in there and surround yourself with every bit of protection you can think of?

Sure, it's a scary world and a lot of ominous things happen around you. But I'd had cake and tea with Ma, and I was back safe in my nice little home, and there were six new orders on my computer. Okay, they were only for Day of Judgment coffee mugs, but tomorrow I'd probably get something bigger and happier.

It wouldn't hurt me to try a little harder with Ma, either. We squabble a lot, but maybe I've been forgetting her good heart, and how much she loves me. For example, after she read some medical news a while back, she planted a yew tree on the grave plot she'd thoughtfully bought in advance so I wouldn't have to worry about it.

You'll always have plenty of tamoxifen if you ever get breast cancer, she said. Now that's a mom although you might just say, as a bona-fide, card-carrying liberal, she doesn't have a whole lot of confidence in the health insurance system in the United States.

Bless her heart, she brought me up to take care of myself. When I was a little kid and I got hit by a car. I said to her, "Ma, where was my guardian angel?"

"Guardian angel? You don't need a guardian angel. When you're strong, like us, you don't *get* a guardian angel."

I remember that on days like this, when I stumble through life with menacing signs from morning to night, and it helps me to cope when Ma's getting on my back a little too much about my lifestyle.

So a little later I called her up and told her I loved her; furthermore, I said I didn't mind a blind date with her girlfriend's son, the accountant. Who knows, it might be a good sign. I like to buy and sell, but keeping the books is a pain in the bazonga.

As I drifted off to sleep, I thought about the directions I'd received from signs that day, depressing and otherwise. I still had faith in my business, but maybe Ma was right about the hot air balloon Jesus. At three thousand bucks, I had a popsicle's chance in Hades of ever selling it to anybody, so I might as well take it downashore on the weekend and try out hot air balloon water skiing.

Maybe it would inspire a whole bunch of people and I'd be on TV that night.

"It was reliably reported that a six-story tall Jesus swooped down on the New Jersey shore this weekend and scooped up one water skier, supposedly the only person worth saving in the Rapture."

That means there's gonna be a hell of a lot of disappointed Born-Again Christians in New Jersey, every one of them a potential customer for my website. On the spot, I invented something new, got it in production the next day, and it's already one of my best sellers: a nice matching panties-and-bra set printed with "The Rapture—Next Year in New Jersey!"

What the hell, how can anybody get through any kind of a life at all without the help of godly gadgets?

Technical Manuals Aren't Written Very Well, Are They?

SINCE MY DAYS WERE occupied with microbiology, for relaxation I took a night-school course in bonsai. Not intellectually demanding, but still, a feeling of satisfaction. Work at the lab was going every which way. My colleagues were conspiring to knife me in the back, and it was nice to feel some control in my private life.

I settled on an apple tree for my project. Purely mechanical manipulation. Cut and wire the roots to limit intake of nourishment. Same for the branches. Water sparingly. The tree grew to be about a foot tall, and stayed that way. Perfect little tree, nice red apples about the size of blueberries.

I put it in a charming Victorian terrarium that cried out for a complete landscape and using a large irregularly shaped blue bowl, made a nice pool, with the tree on the bank, producing a scene that was peaceful although perhaps somewhat static.

A glittering little rainbow trout from the pet store supplied the perfect finishing touch, actually a regular fish that in the wild could grow to be a foot long. All I had to do was stunt its growth by keeping it in a little space. I'd had aquariums before, and I knew creatures grew only as big as the space that accommodated them. You may have heard that giants once walked upon the earth, but there was a lot more open space than there is now.

A little pond with a little fish under a little tree. I'd come home drained from a hellish day in the lab, eat a frozen dinner, and take my glass of wine in beside the terrarium, wave a magazine over the top to watch the leaves blow, and watch the fish swimming around. Tasted one of the little apples, but it was sour as hell and actually made me feel sick. Disappointing. On the whole, however, my little world was a tremendous comfort for some time.

But after a while, I thought how interesting it would be to have *more*. Think about a landscape painting. No matter how pretty the scenery, it always needs some human figures to give it a point. After all, someone's got to appreciate all that green and blue, to be young and happy under the apple bough. This was a bit harder, but I did a clone procedure with some of my own cells, treated at appropriate times with some anti-growth factor.

Don't let anybody tell you this is science. It's art. Totally against a whole lot of federal regulations but it was fun to try out some of the Japanese technology. In the end, no matter how bitter work was making me, I had a pretty little creature curled up in a grassy nest to think about. I accelerated her maturation a bit, and then let her settle down at about eighteen, complete with shapely legs, a nice little rosy bottom, tiny delicate breasts, about two inches tall. I can't begin to tell you how charming she/I was.

Sometimes when I was working on something particularly tricky in the lab, I let my thoughts dwell on the me that was curled up under an apple tree watching a fish and for a few moments felt peace. Maybe I spent my days tied up in knots watching my back, but she only sat cross-legged on the grass, stretched out to take a nap, and ate the tasty bites I left for her lunch. Just thinking about her perfect happiness calmed me.

The next step was inevitable. She needed a companion. Okay, maybe I needed a companion. Maybe I was buying into a story, but I worried about her being alone all the time I was at work. Since she had already been engineered in various ways, it was easiest to use her as a source, so I blew a little anesthetic on her face, and when she was asleep, did a reverse Adam and Eve.

It's not generally known, but all human embryos are female until some get a flood of hormones that turns them male. If it weren't for that, we'd be a female world. All the gestation and tinkering took several months, but then I had a nice two-and-a-half inch, eighteen-year-old partner for her. Looked exactly like me as well.

Voyeurism? Maybe. I knew I'd like to see them having sex, but I'd made up my mind beforehand that I'd have to guide them. If they tried anything kinky, I was going to put a stop to it pretty damn fast. I just wanted a controllable little world to help me cope with the demands of federal funding and my ambitious colleagues. A world where everything was peaceful, the way my own world wasn't.

By mid-summer, I had that. A little pond with a little fish and a little pair of humans under a little tree. They were shy with each other at first, but in a couple of weeks walked around together all the time, curled up with each other to sleep, and shared the shortbread crumbs I dropped them at tea time. I had the same contented feeling I remembered from childhood when I was playing with my dollhouse but a million times better. I felt there was someone waiting for me to come home at night. Totally uncommunicative as yet but my children.

At work, I knew meetings were going on without me and I was being kept out of the loop. Eden, as I had started to call it for short, needed to develop in compensation. For a while it was enough to work on their diet. They seemed happy with any kind of food, but I kept them vegetarian. I liked planning new tastes and leaving treats out for them to discover when they woke up in the morning, like finding an Easter basket every day.

I never wanted them to feel hungry and go foraging, what with those sour, unpleasant apples and the fish just about the only consumable things in their environment. What if they got the munchies and some instinct led them to kill the fish and eat it? The idea of them eating it raw was revolting, so I'd have to teach them about fire, and then they would probably chop the tree down for fuel, leaving them with no protection from the sun when I put the terrarium outside for Vitamin D. Better never to let them get near the idea they could eat other living things. I didn't even want to think about them playing with fire.

I avoided the whole issue by always leaving them plenty of crumbs, bits of cheese and the smaller fruits, which they held in both hands and nibbled. They looked cute down on their hands and knees with their little bottoms in the air sipping from the jar lid I kept filled because I didn't want them drinking the water the fish was in.

I wondered what they thought of the huge hand that came out of nowhere several times a day with tasty vittles. After a while, they came running as soon as the shadow of my hand hovered over their home. It seemed sad, in a way, that their life was tied up with shadows.

Over the next few months, I tinkered. Thought up new items of interest for their little world. Thought how cute a little frog would look there beside the pond with the little fish. No sooner said than done. Really wanted birds but they wouldn't stay in the tree. Before I knew what was happening, they were out in the room, and so I just let them out the window.

The tiny kitten and puppy I made worked a lot better. They went wild over them, and with my connections in the molecular biology community, I got the raw materials, and pretty soon they had little giraffes, elephants and some interesting hybrids I made to see what would happen. I didn't give them any carnivores because (1) I didn't want to put that violence into their minds and (2) it's more work than you realize to make these things. Made a note to see if I could get some of that dinosaur DNA from fossil bones. Non-carnivorous ones, of course.

I realized that, with all my embellishments, their little Garden of Eden was becoming too small. Adam and Eve didn't have enough space for exercise. In the beginning, sometimes I carried them around like two-legged gerbils, put them in my shirt pocket, and we'd go for a walk in the cool of the evening. However, after a heart-stopping experience with a cat in the park at the end of my street, I made a pen for them in my back yard and let them run to their hearts' content. That would be fine until the next winter came.

In the end I just took over the spare bedroom, which I only used as a place to throw my out-of-season clothes. Spread plastic on the floor and brought in nice garden soil, a bucket at a time because I no longer had time to go to the gym, and my back was starting to give me problems again. Threw on some of that new grass seed that stays short and bought a sunlamp.

After I finished the first grassy bit, I scooped them up out of the terrarium and let them watch me finish their world. For a while they just stayed there, and I was worried they wouldn't be able to adjust, but after their initial shyness, they were running all over touching everything, and I felt like a proud parent.

I could see they were intelligent because they watched everything I did with their bright little eyes and even touched each other on the arm and pointed when I did something particularly interesting to them, like putting in additional bonsai trees I'd bought at the Japanese nursery.

I realized I had to reserve a space for me to use when I was overseeing them, so I left one section near the door without any garden and brought in a comfortable armchair, a lamp, and a table. They pretty much avoided that area, and I decided not to play with them while I was sitting there. That was my observation post. I hoped after a while they would get used to it and forget about me so I could watch them when they thought they were alone. Maybe they never thought that, big figure like me looming over in the corner, but look at how we get used to the sun.

The time had come to work on issues beyond the basics. Regardless of their size, they were human beings, and I needed to teach them the things all humans know. One night, after I'd finished a bottle of Châsse Du Pape, I announced to them in the same way I would have talked to a cat, "I am not the lord your god but I'm here to help you."

They looked blank and a little scared. Of course I knew they didn't understand words yet, and anyway they must have just heard a big rumble like a voice of thunder. For the first time, I had a little doubt and wondered if I couldn't have had just about as much fun getting into a really elaborate dollhouse, where all I would have to do was pick up the dolls and move them from the library to the drawing room. Now I had no option but to move ahead.

The whole issue of communication had been skipped over in the big book of cautionary tales. The Chomskian predilection for language must have been better developed in those days, or a whole chunk had been left out.

I realized it would be easier to start with "Yes, you can do that" before going on to "That's a big fat no-no" but I had to give them a vocabulary first, so I went to the library and got some books on teaching language, another thing to master before I could take our relationship up a level or two. Pretty soon realized it was key. Like a lot of DIY projects, this was becoming a hell of a lot more work than I had envisioned.

Enchanted with all the trees and the space, they ignored my efforts to teach them words. I thought, well, I could just let them continue on like gerbils, but there was something in me that wanted them to be everything they could be. After all, they were just like me, only in miniature. Hell, they *were* me. Why shouldn't they have the tools to do anything I could do?

Moreover, they had me to help them learn, and I could make sure they avoided a lot of the pain in life. Food was provided, light came and went regularly, I kept the room nice and warm, like a tropical paradise. No need for clothes. Conceivably, they could eventually produce works of art (in miniature, of course) that surpassed anything in the Louvre.

I toyed with the idea of gradually working them up through all the ages—first neolithic, then medieval, eighteenth century with those silky clothes and elaborate wigs. However, I thought it was demeaning to their dignity to use them like a theme park. Moreover, they'd probably get very confused and their language skills weren't going to be good enough for psychoanalysis for a long time, so I didn't entertain that idea very long.

Since they weren't interested in language at all, I decided I had to use some old-fashioned methods. I couldn't keep their attention long enough to make them pay attention to any of my word modeling, as recommended by the language teaching books I'd got from the library, so I took a cue from Pavlov.

The first time, they looked puzzled when I put supper down and immediately removed it, lids filled with buttered mashed potatoes mixed with cheese, same as I was having, one of their favorites. As soon as they came running up, I took the food away and said in the softest voice I could, "Supper." It took them a long time to get the first word out but they finally did, and I put the chow down.

After that, we zipped through a nice program of naming their environment. I thought it would be cute to let them give new names to the animals in the garden, but they had problems getting the idea that they were allowed to invent names, and in the interest of saving time I taught them the standard words. I was dreading the work we had ahead of us on abstract concepts.

Almost while I was thinking of that, Adam, who was a much faster eater, reached over and scooped up a big handful of Eve's spuds. It was the moment. I almost said "Bad Adam," but I stopped myself in time, scooped up Adam in my hand, shook him a little, looked him in his little eyes and said in a very loud, displeased voice, "SIN." When I put him down again, he made it a point to get as far away from the supper dish as he could while Eve finished up.

After a while, they were pretty conversant, and almost every evening we talked, although not on a very elevated level yet. I used a little mike near them, and I learned to whisper-talk. It was pretty good most of the time unless I got excited and boomed, and then I saw them wince and put their hands over their ears.

Sometimes, especially on those days I had to stay late at the lab and still felt I had to carry on with the little evening chats they had grown used to, I thought this must be just like having children. You pick them up from daycare after your day's work, feed them, give them baths, read them the bedtime story.

I thought how much my Adam and Eve had to learn, just as children do, and for the first time, sadly realized they would grow old and die. Small creatures often have faster metabolisms. Would my little alter egos die in two or three years, having grown old? Would I have to build them little coffins and read the prayers for the dead over them? I hadn't thought of any of this when I created them. Watching them die would be like having one of my limbs amputated.

Lazy little beggars, though. I kept their paradise going, but I thought they should learn a good work ethic, and so I made some little knives and rakes and taught them to cut the grass, gave them some seeds and made them do a little elementary gardening. They slacked off every chance they got to roll in the grass and take the naps they loved.

I thought of a puppet show, made paper dolls called Adam and Eve to act out morality tales. This worked pretty well and so every evening we had a sort of Mr. Rogers program where I taught them about right and wrong, the dignity of work, and some basic ideas about problem-solving.

Sexuality hadn't poked its ugly head up yet but, like most eighteen-year-olds, Adam was walking around most of the time with an erection. I saw Eve poking at it, so I thought it was just a matter of time. Spent a lot of time writing a whole series of puppet shows on morality and ethics, went through a basic sex education class with them, and then one Friday evening I taught them how. Made a nice little nest of soft grass with a silky scarf over it and fixed a snack for them to have after. Brie on crackers, lemon square fragments, a little mound of tiramisu, and a very small lid of Cabernet.

Picked Adam up and put him on top of Eve. She started to squirm and hit him, so I had to say "SIN" to her, and she quieted down. Then he was sulking and didn't want to have anything to do with her. It took some time.

I put them both in the palm of my hand, used a feather to ease her legs apart, settled him in between, and after a while, the deed was done. They just sort of lay there looking happy, and I put the snacks down. Maybe I shouldn't have inaugurated such an elaborate ritual, but I wanted their wedding night to be something wonderful for them to remember.

In bed that night I regretted I hadn't taught them about clothes yet because I could have made Eve a pretty wedding dress and taught them about ceremonies, but still I went to sleep happy thinking I had brought joy to the little creatures.

It was kind of neat, however, how I could tell when they were thinking about sex and stop it dead by sternly saying "SIN."

Best word I ever taught them. They picked it up themselves. Caught them more than once starting to dally and one or the other would say "sin?" and look upwards. I think they thought sin was synonymous with sex and made a note to myself to try to straighten that out since I realized how I had contributed to their confusion.

Sometimes when they started to caress each other, I would pick them up and put them together. At other times (I admit it, when the lab had been particularly oppressive), I would say "SIN" in a dreadful voice. Double attraction-avoidance situation.

Work was getting stressful. Although most of the time I was very good to them, I realized I was taking it out on my little creatures. The double messages did come back to haunt me later, and I've often wished I'd thought their education out more thoughtfully instead of just flying by the seat of my pants.

More and more I found myself taking short cuts. Originally I had thought I would break all new ground, invent a totally new system of philosophy and religion for them, but when I was faced with teaching them after a stressful day, fairy tales and even the Big Book offered efficacious ways of getting points across.

After Adam used his little grass-cutting knife to make some exploratory pokes at the cord of my lamp, fortunately causing sparks but not killing himself, I thought I'd better put a little more emphasis on obedience. I decided to tell them that under no circumstances were they ever to touch the lamp that stood beside my chair. Used the "S" word and a few other scary tactics to drive the lesson home.

After all, I didn't want them to get pushy and want to control the sun, the moon, and the stars. I liked having that light there so I could sit in my chair and watch them explore, so I put their little hands on the electric cord and then used "SIN" in the major booming thunder voice they didn't like and left them in the dark for a while. I noticed after that they cut a wide swathe around my whole area.

The opportunity came for me to spend a long weekend in the Virgin Islands. I couldn't see any reason not to go if I left them plenty of food and water and put the light on a timer. I felt a little uneasy that they would get bored, and so I went to a pet shop and bought a bunch of toys. Usually sex was enough to occupy them, but I was getting a little annoyed that they were having so much when I wasn't having any.

I thought some distractions would do them good, so I picked up an exercise wheel with tinkling bells and a parakeet mirror that should really intrigue them since I realized they had never seen themselves. The best was a very funny battery-operated SpongeBob SquarePants that came with a supply of twenty words and expressions that were tripped off when they walked near it. I thought they might as well learn something while they were being amused. I put the toys down and stayed nearby while they got used to them. Everything seemed pretty cool, and I left for several well-deserved days of rest and relaxation.

They were there on my mind more than I would have thought while I was gone. I wondered if they'd be like the Sims, that carried on in their computer world when you didn't have time to log on. Flying home, I was as eager to see them as I would have been if they were kids. I'd brought back a souvenir box of pralines and thought I'd give them a whole one instead of crumbs to see if they would gorge until they were sick or self-monitor.

The best-laid plans oft gang agley, as the poet put it, or in modern vocabulary, SNAFU (situation's normal, all fucked up). When I walked in and flicked the switch, nothing. I hadn't predicted a blown fuse and the poor little things had spent four days in darkness because I'd drawn the shades before I left. They must have been terrified, left all alone, and then the light going like the end of the world. Once I got the fuse replaced, I went in with a lid of cream and a splash of brandy to try to soothe them.

The whole landscape was rearranged. It must have taken a lot of trips to build their dirt hill with just the acorn tops I'd been teaching them to drink from. There were skid marks where they'd somehow pushed and pulled SpongeBob SquarePants up to the top. I realized they were trying to placate him, and I felt like crying, but then I got enraged when I saw the soggy disintegrating remains of the fish, the first little being in my creation, that they'd pulled out of the pond and deposited in front of him.

And where were they? Over in the corner, behind some miniature terrarium plants, fucking for all they were worth. They were so involved with each other they didn't even realize I'd come in. Him on top, her on top, sideways, upside down, all where they thought SpongeBob wouldn't be able to see them. Anyway, hadn't they given him a fish to keep him happy?

Some sort of invented orgiastic ceremony in their own little Sodom and Gomorrah. There was no other way to describe it. Where had it come from? Nothing I'd taught them unless it was the puppet shows. I felt guilty I'd given them SpongeBob, but I'd thought he was cute, the way the voices came out when you got near, and well, I thought he'd be company when I wasn't there.

I was on the verge of tears. What good had it done to try so hard, make everything so nice, give them only the tiniest minimum of restriction, and that only for their own good, if the minute they were left alone they got in trouble?

I got down on my hands and knees and shoved my huge angry face in front of them. I wanted them to feel as bad as I did.

"SIN," I shouted, in the loudest voice I had.

"SIN, SIN, SIN! YOU NASTY LITTLE CREATURES! YOU RATS! YOU SINNERS! I HATE YOU AND I DON'T EVEN WANT TO SEE YOU ANYMORE! ABOMINATION! SIN! SIN!"

They shuddered and hid as deep as they could get in the shrubbery.

I'd got myself in a mess. I had a couple of scotches and thought how I could get rid of the horrible little things. I forgot they were me and just thought of them as clever rodents.

I knew the time had come to dismantle the world. It had gotten out of hand. It was an unbelievable mess. There was no way I would have time to be god or even not-god. Teaching them, even un-teaching them, would be an enormous undertaking. They were insatiable. Everything I taught them led to the need for more.

They spoke quite well now, and I'd already started giving them an oral tradition. Soon I'd have to teach them to read and write and make little books for them. Get them a dollhouse probably. Little clothes. Little furniture. Little appliances. Little telephones and computers. Why should I spend all my time doing this?

I could see the writing on the wall. They would need every minute of the rest of my life. It was just a matter of time before there was a whole bunch of little Cains and Abels. I'd thought Eve was looking plump lately, which wouldn't have been at all unusual considering the way they went at it all the time. There was bipolar, schizophrenia, and sociopathy on both sides of my family, and it hadn't been diluted by your ordinary sexual reproduction. Those kids were going to be a mess.

They'd consume my days, and I'd had an offer from Berkeley so I could leave the horrors of my present job. I supposed I could take them with me in some sort of cat carrier but, I'm sorry, I was tired of the whole mess. I wanted to start over fresh without any responsibilities.

They were a hell of a lot bigger than they used to be, too, and muscular. In my enthusiasm to make them happy in their room-world, I'd forgotten about the space limitation rule. As long as they were confined in the terrarium, they stayed a nice size, about two inches high. After they had their fine big world to roam in, they grew inexorably bigger. Four inches, six inches, before I knew it, they were eight inches tall and growing.

I knew I should drown them while I could still hold them down, but after I'd filled the tub and had them squirming in my hands, I couldn't do it. They were so clearly terrified, screaming in their tiny little voices, which somehow made the screaming so much worse.

Finally, I shoved them in my gym bag and dumped them in the park. I left some provisions nearby—a peanut butter and jelly sandwich, an apple, some double-mint oreos, whatever I could grab quick in the kitchen. After that, they'd have to live on seeds or whatever. When I remembered my dear little fish that they'd sacrificed to SpongeBob, I didn't give a damn. I washed my hands of them. The best thing would probably be for them to die, but when I left they were looking around with interest.

Life in California is better than I ever thought it would be. I go out with my colleagues to a variety of ethnic restaurants, and I'm dating a guy ten years younger who is a stockbroker by day and at night plays bass in a retro-grunge group. Bonsai is very popular here, but for my self-improvement I'm staying away from any kind of gardening and taking tennis lessons.

Yeah, I feel guilty about what I did. Sometimes I dream about them. I can't think they'd have made it on their own, especially now that the east has had some really bad winters, but I have to go to a conference there in a couple of months, and I have a feeling I'm not going to be able to resist taking a walk through the park. Who knows, they might see me.

I don't think they'd come running up. After all, we've been apart for some time now. I still shudder to think about the SpongeBob thing and what other idolatrous rituals they might have managed to come up with. If my theory about their life spans was correct, it might even be a new generation now.

But if my Adam and Eve taught their children language and told them about the time they spent with me, who knows, maybe they'll have some second-hand memories of the good old days at 211 Paradise Avenue, and it might give the kids some kind of a feeling to know I'm still around.

On the C Bus

WELL, WE WERE BOTH on the early downtown bus, riding down to the Social Security. We feel better in the morning so we can walk that extra block before the bus turns the corner and be sure of getting a seat. It's a long ride, about forty minutes considering all the stops, especially when you get to that ugly torn-up section around City Hall where they've been working on repairs for years.

We don't get out of the neighborhood that often, so I thought I would make an outing out of it, and I got two nice Danish the night before to eat on the way. Like a picnic, you know. I put them in cellophane bread wrappers to keep them nice and moist and just tucked them into my purse that morning, so Edgar didn't see. Then I planned to say to him, casual-like, after we'd been on the bus about ten minutes, I thought I'd say, wouldn't a Danish taste good about now.

Fat chance of that, unless all of a sudden the downtown bus's got deli service, he'd say. Then I planned I'd say something cheerful that would make him feel it was kind of festive having Danish right while we went down Broad Street, like saying, the C Bus deli, at your service, and pulling out the Danish.

It was mild on Thursday, you remember, not like it was March the third at all. I was trying to make some conversation that morning, and I said, as mild as it is, I think I'll take a chance and wear my spring coat. I'd had a feeling I might wear it, and I'd got it out of the plastic bag I keep it in and hung it out the window all night to get the smell of mothballs out. The land-lord gets very angry if tenants hang things out the window, but our bedroom's on the air shaft, you know, so I thought I would be pretty safe and nobody said a word to me so I judged that pretty well.

He didn't answer, but I knew he was feeling springtime in his heart, too, when I saw he was all dolled up in his two-tone brown-and-white shoes and his double-breasted suit that I got him for our fiftieth from The Second Time Around.

I said, to give him a kick, I don't know if I'm going to let you out looking like that with so many eligible women around, and he just sort of grunted the way he does, but I could tell he was pleased with himself because he made a real effort and said you don't need to carry that cane today, I'll be right beside you all the time.

He was saying I wasn't old enough to need it, you see, but I was scared to take a chance. It's real lightweight, not heavy at all, aluminum, with four little prongs near the ground and good rubber ends. My legs go weak sometimes and even though he said I wouldn't need it, he always says don't hang on me, woman, it drives me crazy, so I didn't want to take a chance.

I put on my navy. A little light, even considering the tempera-ture that day, but I always feel so nice in it. My spring coat's red, so they look stylish together. I remember my mom saying, you can't go wrong with a nice navy, and white gloves, but I used my winter gloves, black, because once my hands get cold, they'll give me twinges for days. I said, trying to keep up a cheerful mood, what they need to invent is nice little hot water bottles you can slip in your pockets, but he just said Christ, and I could tell he wasn't in a very good mood, so I concentrated on getting ready in good time.

His legs have stayed a lot stronger than mine, so I told him to walk on ahead and he could get a newspaper at the stand and save me a place in line. I can't stand all the way downtown and even walking up to an earlier stop doesn't guarantee a seat, so I thought by saying that, he wouldn't feel bad about not liking to poke along with me.

He sat down on one of the seats that face the aisle, up near the driver.

Let's go back to one of the regular seats, I said.

What's wrong with these, he said. Easier to get off. Closer to the door.

Well, I wanted a little privacy for the picnic and the forward-facing seats give me a place to hang my cane, so I said, oh, these seats get so crowded. Everybody tries to squeeze on them. The others are just for two, I said, and he took a deep breath and followed me back a little farther and slid in beside me. We got settled in, and I got that nice warm feeling you get when you've finally got where you're going to go.

Everything had gone okay, I thought, we were both dressed up, and we'd had time for a nice cup of instant coffee, and we'd made the walk and got on the bus, and there were plenty of seats.

I planned to ride along for a couple of blocks before I said wouldn't a Danish taste good, so that's what I did. It worked out just like I thought. He said, Christ, no chance of that here, and I said, C Bus deli at your service and got the Danish out.

Well, I got them out of my bag and gave one to each of us, but just then a lot of people got on. I'm sure glad we got seats, I said, but he was turned around in his seat, and I didn't think he'd heard me. I looked at where he was looking, and I didn't know what to think. He was staring at the woman who was standing right beside our seat.

She was one of those . . . you know. Oh, I didn't have a doubt in the world. Then, before I could even take in what was going on, he sort of half got out of his seat, right beside me, and said to her, would you like this seat? Still holding his Danish!

You bet I would, honey, she said, and then he got up and she sat down. My heart was beating so fast. I didn't know where to look. I couldn't think Edgar would get up and leave me like that, especially to sit beside someone like her. I just rode along in a sort of confusion for two or three blocks.

There aren't any dividers on those seats, and I was squashed up right against her. I felt overwhelmed with the heat from her body and the smell. You could smell the scent on her, why, the whole bus was full of it. It was like a tigress who'd spent the night lying on a bed of jungle flowers, crushing them, until the heavy exotic juices had soaked in her fur and came rushing through the air around her.

Glad to sit down, she said, been on my feet all night, she said, throwing her head back and roaring with laughter, all her big strong white teeth showing in a perfect arch and her soft pink tongue. You're the first man's invited me to *sit* down, she said.

Well, I just sat there. To tell the truth, I felt all mixed up. I'd never in my life been that near anyone like her, and yes, I was afraid of her, and I felt like I might cry because she made me feel old and grey. She just had on some sort of a skimpy little jacket that hardly covered her, but I could feel the heat radiating out of her body.

Oh, it was so strange. I felt as if I were sitting next to an open fire. Sitting there, next to her, I felt . . . somehow . . . oh, I don't know . . . it's so fanciful. . . . oh, I'll say it right out. Even though I knew what she was, I felt a closeness, a safety . . . I felt stronger, as if I didn't need a cane, as if I were warm . . . and brown and peach and gold . . . strong.

I felt sorry for Edgar. He tried so hard, saying with a silly smile, do you always work nights? She just threw back her head and laughed again, shaking her body and stomping her feet up and down, all the movement releasing more of the musky, exotic smell of flowers until I felt giddy with warmth and scent.

I sure do, honey, she said, and now I'm headin' home to crawl in between my sheets, all alone.

Well, as I said, sitting beside her put me in a very strange frame of mind, and when she said that, it was like a vision, as if I were seeing what was in her mind. I saw the bed she was going to, so tall that it was like it was an altar, glittering brass like gold, snowy sheets trimmed in lace, piles of soft, plump pillows, the downy cover glowing in the sun splashing through the windows, colors of sherry wine, and old burgundy, emerald and copper, turned down into the purity and warmth, and, it's hard to say, maybe I should keep this to myself, but I felt myself crawling in beside her and the heat and fragrance plumping me out until I was one with her, and then sleeping through the heat of the day until dusk roused me to eat a meal of thick, rare meat.

I seldom touch flesh, you know, so that was quite strange. If I fill up on vegetables and good bread and butter, there's always enough meat for Edgar, and I really don't require it.

It sounds so odd telling it. I hardly knew whether I should be rude and make a pretext to leave or snuggle up and be closer to her no matter what anyone thought. Not that I would ever have done that, of course, but you know how a thought will just go through your head. I didn't know what to do or how to act, so I pretended to look out through the window, but I could hear everything.

Pretty tired, I guess, he said.

Uh-huh, she said.

I guess you must meet a lot of people, he said, with slyness in his voice, and uh-huh, she said again, not sounding much interested.

May I say how lovely your perfume is?

That's no perfume, old man, she said, and I looked around in alarm and I could see how Edgar whitened at that "old man."

What you smell is me, she said, and I felt like saying something cutting to show her how it felt to be hurt, and I started to think over what I could say.

Then I heard him saying, well, I'm not used to women who smell so fine. My wife, as you can probably smell, seems to favor a perfume called eau de moth balls, and he gave a little laugh.

I just kept looking out the window, not believing he would betray me like that, holding the Danish as if I had just sort of forgotten I had it but might take a bite at any minute.

I felt her shifting her weight in the seat, turning around so she could look at me, and I didn't let on I noticed a bit, but as she moved, the heat of her thigh enveloped mine and I felt warmth throughout my body.

A good smell, she said. I know it well. It's a smell of preservation, of those who guard and keep. I remember well my own granny that raised me. When I smell that smell, I feel safe and loved.

Well, when she was talking about me, I kept feeling safer and warmer. Even my hands got warm.

Then Edgar tried again. My good wife had the brilliant idea to have a picnic on the bus, he said. That is how I come to be riding down Broad Street holding a Danish. Why, I wonder if I might offer you this fresh, untouched pastry, he said, and he sounded so gallant.

Why not, I thought. Neither of us is going to eat them. Putting them into my purse an hour ago seemed in another world, another time. I thought I'd never buy Danish again.

No, thank you, she said. She turned to me, and I looked at her. The breath she exhaled was like gardenias. No, thank you kindly, she said.

She looked at mine, nearly gripped in two where my fingers had clutched it. I looked in her eyes and saw candles burning. She looked at me, and then at the bread, and then she smiled a question at me, and I understood.

Yes, I nodded. Yes, yes, yes, and her soft, warm hands full of heat were gently opening mine and taking the Danish. I saw the dewy, rosy lips open and slowly close on the fruited bread, and my hands glowed, and they've been warm all day.

Our stop came before hers and in the crowded bus, she couldn't move to let me out so I slipped over her, for a moment my body echoing hers like spoons laid in a drawer, and then I was out, in the aisle and then on the sidewalk, walking in the coolness until it was with surprise I saw Edgar walking beside me, and I reached over and held his stiff, cold hand in mine until it gave up and let me warm it.

Demon Love Story

AFTER ALL THOSE YEARS of sex with Satan, so many years of his dry husky embraces, freezing cold until your blood heats them, you've forgotten how warm a real man is, especially when you've come in chilled to the party from one of those late fall nights when your breath is starting to be frosty and even your hair feels chilly as, laughing, you take off your coat in the hall and after you're introduced, he first wraps you in his arms close against him, and then pulls you down the hall and into bed before you've had time to warm up at the hissing old-fashioned radiators.

That starts at a party thrown by the cinematographers who are in town for the film festival. You've invited Satan to go with you but he says he has a headache, you should go and enjoy yourself, so you do. Before you leave the party, you wrap up some garlic-stuffed mushroom caps, blini with caviar, and tiny hazelnut creampuffs in a napkin to take home to Satan. When your new lover catches you, you grin and say they're for your boyfriend.

After that, until you move on to someone else, you meet your new interest every day for lunch and love when you're supposed to be at your yoga lesson. You've lived with Satan so long that you've forgotten what it's like to be with someone who agrees yes, you *should* spend all that money to fly to Japan, where a heretofore unknown director's cut of Toshiro Mifune's *Seven Samurai* has surfaced, and rumor has it the opening is going to feature sake ice cream and carelessly cleaned fugu fish.

Satan has said his contacts told him there was going to be a huge nuclear terrorist attack in Tokyo, and so he wouldn't spring for the ticket.

Satan hasn't made an effort for years, not since he conquered you at fourteen by dangling a goth rock recording contract in front of your eyes and bankrolled the recordings, the world tours, the mansion with an Olympic-size swimming pool and all the hashish you wanted.

Now, at twice that age, you've been replaced on MTV by other fourteen-year-olds, and you've stopped smoking anything. A purseful of charge cards isn't a lot of consolation when you've got a spring-and-winter marriage, and Satan does nothing but hang around the house hinting for you to fix him tomato soup and toasted cheese sandwiches while he watches daytime cable.

After the first one, infidelity follows you easily. You catch yourself looking all the time.

A pair of strong legs with golden hair in shorts and construction boots. You fall in the construction trailer at lunch time.

A pale young man with one dark lock falling onto his forehead and a slim volume of Cole Swenson shoved in his pocket. You fall on a wooden chair deep in the stacks at the University of Pennsylvania where you've gone to get some books on the Inquisition for Satan.

When you hear about a priest who always knows when he has a suicide in his confessional and gives an especially loving blessing, you go with a list so damning he's reluctant to let you leave, says you need spiritual direction, so the two of you go back to the rectory, where he makes hot chocolate with real cream and a splash of brandy. It's inevitable that you fall.

For a long time, you still go back to the apartment afterward, moist between your legs and glowing with love. Satan always has some nice little snacks fixed for you, the kettle hot to make herbal tea. While he fusses around warming the teapot, he keeps asking if you still love him, and you say of course with your fingers crossed behind your back.

While he's been waiting for you, he's been wrapped up in the granny square afghan your mother made, watching old movies on the Nostalgia Channel. Now, since you're way overheated, his cold body feels refreshing as you go to sleep, and he starts on Conan.

It grows harder to keep up your double life. You're in a sailors' bar down on the waterfront when you meet the best one you've ever met. He can touch all your hot buttons like no one before. It's like he knows everything about you. It's like he *is* you. The epitome of lovers, all the characteristics of all the others all rolled up in one. It's as exciting as it was when you first met Satan, even accounting for the fact that then you were naive, and now you've been around the block a few times. You think this is the one who is meant for you, the one you can spend the rest of your life with, and you decide to leave Satan.

After several hours of warm firm love, your new lover knows to have a plate of Krispy Kreme doughnuts and two glasses of your favorite Cabernet waiting, the glasses filled too full, with his characteristic abundance, causing the wine to bell up slightly with surface tension at the level of the rim so that the slightest touch of your lips, as you bend over to take the first sip of the glass too full to lift, causes a few drops to run down the outside of the glass and be swept up with your tongue tip.

Nothing like Satan who's gotten so he saves the good bottles for the company you never have and buys jug wine and even boxes for everyday.

Although life with Satan has become sad and boring, for some time you've kept up your interest in goth rock, which after all was where you made your mark. You're still a little famous, and sometimes you see one of your videos on afternoon MTV, on the type of program that shows early Michael Jackson and sometimes even the Monkees.

Now it seems like too much effort. You don't bother to accept an invitation to open the new used-CD store that's come into the neighborhood and wants a few has-beens for a little free publicity.

You let all the exotic birds in the conservatory go free and call the caretakers to come over to empty the pool and drape it in the end-of-the-season cloth.

You begin to eat oatmeal for breakfast and clean up your language.

For years Satan has ordered all your clothes from catalogues that come in plain brown wrappers—red and black satin, monkey fur from species so new they don't even have names yet. Your closets are stuffed to bursting with costumes for every century, bustiers and fish-net stockings and the entire stock of left-over costumes from *Tom Jones* that he got at an online auction.

You bundle them all up and leave them at the Salvation Army thrift shop.

Now you dress in surreptitiously bought pale silks and cashmeres, meet other softspoken girls with ash-blonde hair carelessly piled on top of their heads and escaping in soft tendrils that curl down their slender necks for coffee and cakes in pastel salons where you pile the extra chairs with shopping bags of fragrant purchases reverently wrapped in tissue paper by slender middle-aged clerks who live with their mothers and work in pearl-grey-carpeted department stores where the eponymous sad pianist gently plays Satie, and you talk about love.

Not a place where the memory of dry husky skin and inarticulate second-language-learner speech should, could intrude.

You ask Satan to move out and he goes away, but he isn't letting you go that easily. When you come back from an evening of welcoming your lover's warmth into your body and go to draw the shades before sinking your exercised and musky body into sandalwood and bubbles, you see him standing grey and loveless under the street light, his horny skin glistening from drops of midnight rain.

On your birthday, you're awakened at dawn by the happy music of the Mexican mariachi band he has ordered to bring you a serenade, and later a delivery truck brings you a chihuahua puppy curled up in a sombrero. A take-out meal of enchiladas suizas, margaritas and caramel bread pudding is delivered by donkey.

You wonder why Satan has thought an ethnic birthday might bring you back to him, but you write a thank-you note and fasten it to the street light with duct tape. You stand at the window and watch him read it, but when he looks hopefully up at the window, you shake your head and go to bed.

As you go to sleep, you know he's still there and know when you wake up early and go down to the corner cafe, he'll be at the counter with a cinnamon-raisin bagel, a cappuccino and an unread newspaper lying before him, looking at you from the corners of his eyes with that terrible humble quality *I know I'm not good enough for you but please please please let me come back.*

It's hard to order your almond croissant and your double latte to go.

The day comes when you haven't seen him for so many weeks that you think he's finally found some other fourteen-year-old and gone away, but you've forgotten Satan's cunning that made him Prince of Darkness over the whole world.

You're lying numb from relaxation in bed watching your new lover, who knows to order matching bottles of Château La-tour 82 for lunch, one beside your plate and the other beside his, who has a pilot's license and puts the plane on automatic while he plays the guitar and recites Rumi, the one you thought maybe was the one for you for the rest of your life.

He slips for a minute when he's pulling on his shirt, hand-made of the finest Egyptian cotton, and greedily drinking his body in, you see the scar from the amputated tail at the base of his spine, and you realize your lazy, slipping-into-middle-age, tomato-soup-and-toasted-cheese Satan still has a few tricks in his magician's tall hat.

When he sees you've noticed, he falls on his knees and asks you please to forgive him, tells you he's seen the error of his ways, tells you he wants you so much he's willing to stay warm for your whole lifetime. What can you do? He's figured out you're a sucker for romance.

You fall again and gently, shyly, tell your new lover you think maybe now he can come home again.

He accepts happily and suggests going together to Ethan Allen to buy some new furniture, including a few sets of slipcovers so you can have a new look often. You have to work to keep a rela-tionship alive, he says, we have to be constantly growing, constantly evolving. Let's shake things up, have a whole new look, hell, even a whole new way of being. But I don't think we need a TV, do you, he says anxiously, I think they take the romance away from a relationship.

Because you love him, you relent and say you think he could have a small non-smart TV for the news and weather, but definitely not satellite and probably not even high-definition cable.

You send a little prayer to heaven for your newfound wisdom and say you'll slip down to the lobby to get him a Sunday paper for the ads.

You might stop at the bar for a quick nightcap, you say, but you'll be back before he finishes his evening programs, absolutely.

Who Do You Say I Am?

Matthew 16: 13–20

YOU'VE GATHERED IN CHURCH to wait for Jesus. Unarguable signs have let you know this is the day. This is the day of the second coming. This is Judgment Day.

It was a no-brainer to wait at the church. There was more discussion over whether it should be a potluck but in the end everybody agreed a collection of simple dishes appropriate for Lent would be okay and a blessing to the elderly and fragile. Many of you have gone across the street to that expensive little shop that sells home-cooked frozen gourmet meals, more expensive than doing it yourself but so convenient.

You've all spent quite a bit of time deciding what to wear, trying to steer the line between too casual, which could be interpreted as disrespectful, and too formal, which could lead a suddenly silent Jesus to add up and look askance at your well-fitting suit and silk turtleneck.

There are examples of both approaches present. Most seem to have chosen the middle way, stuff you could pick up at The Gap or J. Crew—natural fabrics, cotton, wool, linen—but nothing ostentatious, the sort of clothing you might wear for a Parent-Teacher Association meeting. You've left your gold jewelry at home. Except for watches. Somehow you want to keep track of time.

You're sitting in a circle of chairs left over from the meeting on Sunday about whether or not the church's present predilection to elect gay bishops and even women was going to hasten the end of the world. That was before the announcement about the end coming, so some thought it had, and others said it was just coincidence.

On the whole, those present seem to have borrowed their attitudes and voice tones from old funerals. There is surreptitious glancing at the watches as the morning goes on. Occasionally someone answers a cell phone but talks in a low, well-bred voice.

Everybody is longing for a cup of coffee, but nobody likes to give in and actually go start the dripping. What if Jesus walked in when you had the steaming cup in your hand, tantalizing your nostrils, but before you'd actually brought the cup to your lips? What if such addiction to worldliness counted against you? What if then you were sent over with the goats and had to put the cup down carefully on the table near the door, having gone to the trouble of making coffee but never having had your last sip?

These and other small issues are on everyone's mind.

The group has started the waiting with several nice prayers but then silence ensues. You are all wondering if there will be a sign, something like a mass ringing of bells, a clap of thunder, or brazen and echoing angel voices to get things started. Might Gabriel actually appear as the advance man to give you time for a last bathroom call, time to uncross your legs, straighten ties, clasp hands demurely in your laps?

This is doomed not to be.

You all start at the sound of the door opening and closing. There is some banging and cursing and the sounds of someone or something falling. The same thought comes to everyone's mind—all those stacked-up contributions for the thrift shop. Then someone limps and scrapes down the hall. You've just relaxed when that someone comes in the door. This person is bizarre enough that you know something is up. You can't believe it, but in your heart, you know Jesus has arrived.

Short guy, not more than five feet one or two, made worse by his bent and twisted appearance because of the hunched back. Long straggly beard. What hair is left is scruffy and full of dandruff you can see across the room. Squinting at you.

God forgive you, you hope somehow you can be judged from across the room because you can smell the stench already. The room is full of it. He's probably never taken a bath in his life, and he's obviously drunk so much alcohol for so long that he's as full of alcohol fumes as Rappaccini's daughter was full of poison.

Didn't it say, somewhere in Luke, that people said Jesus ate and drank too much, talked about how he preferred old wine to new? Did he have a substance abuse problem even then? Who would have known it was this bad?

Still, he is the Lord. No getting around that, and even his Father said, "My ways are not your ways." Who are we to judge? Better not judge. You've got to remember—judge not lest ye be judged. Judge not, judge not, judge not. Maybe he can read minds. Even if he picks up what you're thinking, he'll know you're struggling against it, and that's got to count.

His robe may have been white once, but now it's full of years of dirt and food stains. You can see the long, jagged fingernails clutching his crutch, and you realize in the midst of winter he's barefoot, and you're horribly aware of his horny, yellow toenails. Oh, yes, his nose is running, and he wipes it on the back of his hand.

He smiles at you, and you realize the smile full of missing and rotten teeth is meant to be sweet and reassuring.

"I guess you've all been waiting for some time. Sorry to be so late. The sidewalks haven't been plowed or even salted yet. Fell down twice. By the way, I think you're in violation of the fire code with all that junk in the hall."

Everybody starts to get up and head toward the door.

"No, no, don't bother to move it now. The time is short."

Alarming. All of you who have been half out of your seats to run out and show the proper spirit by moving the boxes sink back and try to look holy, dismiss the thought of coffee from your minds. You feel like second graders who are all going to be punished because the person who put a tack on teacher's chair won't confess.

He gingerly eases himself into a seat near the door, under the big crucifix, and lays his crutch down beside it. The chair is near a radiator, which magnifies the smell. Silence ensues. You wonder what to do. Is this a test?

Are you supposed to pretend you don't notice what he looks like? Would this show you don't judge people on externals?

Are you supposed to excuse yourself and run down to the restroom, rend your garments, dig some dirt out of the flower-pots and smear yourself up a little, dip your head under the faucet to get the mousse out, appear flat and stringy, and go back into the room barefoot to show solidarity with the suffering people of the world?

Are you supposed to say, diffidently, um, excuse me, I know how busy you've been and probably haven't had time to freshen up. We have a shower in the basement and a supply of clothes from the thrift shop for homeless guests who are in need of them. Would you like someone to show you the way down and where the deodorant and mouthwash are kept? We'll just wait here until you're ready to come back.

Would this show hospitality to strangers, say your hearts are in the right place in spite of the natural fabrics and gold watches?

Which is the right answer?

Increasing visual and olfactory discomfort leads Mrs. Upper, with a consciousness of her responsibility as head of the vestry, to go for the third option, addressing Jesus as Sir, and ask if he'd like to be shown the facilities. You realize with relief that someone has made a decision, and you'e off the hook.

When Jesus says sure, he'd like a chance to freshen up, once he's on his way downstairs, you all dash to the restrooms and scruff yourselves up a bit, pull shirttails out, yank off ties so you can meet in the middle. He'll be a bit tidier, you'll be a bit scruffier. Then you return to the room and sit down to wait. And wait. And wait.

Since things seem to have loosened up a bit, someone puts the coffee on and that fragrant homey scent, plus opening the windows for a while, regardless of the temperature, does quite a bit to freshen the room.

The waiting gets to be a strain, so you're all happy when you hear him coming back. Even his stride seems to indicate the facilities offered have done him good. You whisper, *I think this is going to help quite a lot. I just couldn't see myself being judged by someone who smelled like that.*

You all nod your heads, feeling good you've offered hot water, soap and clean clothes to God.

Then he enters the room, having availed himself of what was offered. In addition to now being clean, he has straightened up and grown a few inches, showered and shaved, seemingly been totally enamored of the lotion and dumped it all over himself, unfortunately using the bottle of drugstore Joy instead of Brut. You would forgive him for not being informed about twenty-first-century fragrances, but his total appearance is still dismaying, and you wish you had the bum back.

He's chosen a nice polyester cocktail dress in lime and magenta complemented by a sequined powder blue sweater and some six-inch spike-heeled gold strappy sandals. I thought I told you to throw those out, someone whispers. Jesus smiles at the person, and he says he's glad she didn't because now he can see over the heads of the crowd.

The beard is gone, and he has inexpertly moussed his hair and fluffed it up. He's used too much and it's spiked like the Statue of Liberty. His makeup is far too bright although it's a pleasure to see his gleaming white teeth and beautifully manicured nails, done the new way with little miniature pictures on each one. He must have found the stack of fashion magazines and leafed through them.

You're not sure whether you're upset because he seems to have changed gender or because his fashion choices are so tacky.

He sits down right under the big crucifix on the wall and asks if there's any coffee left. One of the vestry rushes to get it for him, bringing the cream and sugar on a tray. He pours in so much cream that the coffee is in danger of spilling over. When he adds a few spoons of sugar, it does slop over on the floor.

"Damn," he says. "Sorry. I've just got such a sweet tooth." He starts to get up.

"I'll get some paper towels from the kitchen."

You say please to let you do it and rush off. When you return, you bring some doughnuts on a plate, left over from the meeting to talk about the Bishop.

Jesus eats the doughnuts, seemingly not noticing they're a little stale, unfortunately spilling powdered sugar that smears when he tries to brush it off his dress, drinks some coffee, then looks around and says, "Well, isn't this nice?"

Everyone nods eagerly, then silence. More silence that goes on until the normal time for lunch. Growling stomachs punctuate the silence.

Finally Jesus speaks again.

"Ummmm, I don't want to rush you" (everybody sits up) "but I do have the whole world to get to, so I wonder if you've made any decisions."

More silence.

Someone finally dares to speak up.

"Decisions? What do you mean?"

"Decisions," he says somewhat impatiently, so you can glimpse the god through the tarty exterior.

"Decisions. This is Judgment Day. You were told two thousand years ago that it was coming. Remember. I told you in these exact words."

Crossing his long graceful legs in their pearly pantyhose and golden sandals, Jesus runs rapidly through all the signs.

"Nation rising against nation, pestilence, famines, earthquakes, false prophets, abominations of holy places, etc. All that's well under way. To be quite honest, I don't even understand why you're here. That's partly why I was late. I spent a lot of time looking for you.

"When you saw all these signs, you were told to flee to the mountains, not stop to take anything with you, not even to go back to the house for your coat. I had to include pregnant women to be fair, but I didn't say you couldn't carry them. Them and the crippled, the old, anybody that needs a little extra accommodation.

"I've been searching all the mountains and as far as I can tell, the only people there are die-hard skiers enjoying the almost-empty lifts. I didn't have the heart to summon them for judgment just yet so they're getting in a last few cold smoke runs in that fresh powder.

"I told you it might be in winter and here it is. I guess you didn't pay attention to any of this. You just kept working, playing, accumulating more stuff, thought your fur coats could keep you warm in *my winter!*"

Realizing he is becoming a bit strident, Jesus leans back again and takes a sip of his coffee before continuing in a voice like a college professor assigned to remedial English.

"Didn't I say to watch for my word becoming widespread? I said, and I quote, concerning this sign, the Savior says: 'And this gospel of the kingdom shall be preached in the whole world, for a testimony to all nations, and then shall the consummation come.'

"Wake up and smell the coffee, folks! It's all over cable any Sunday morning.

"Return of Enoch and Elijah? The Undead Prophets rock band, with singer Enoch and Elijah on bass? They've been having a ball, but I guess you've all been listening to Barry Manilow, which won't count against you. No one will be consigned to hell for their musical taste.

"The Great Apostasy? No one in France has been to church for years, and there are only about fifty Episcopalians left in the United States, probably most of them gathered in this hall.

"Reign of the Anti-Christ? This one should have been a dead giveaway. I can tell you've all been neglecting your numerology or you would have figured out which world leader's name qualifies for the Beast 666. Look here."

Jesus walks over, hips swaying in that way you can't help in six-inch spikes, to the big tablet on an easel used in Sunday school. Selecting a bright purple marker, he draws the following.

"Let's start out by looking at the Hebrew system. Okay, here's the letter values for each letter of his first and last names. Just add up the values for gimel (3), heh (5), ayin (70), resh (200), gimel (3), heh (5), beth (2), ayin (70), shin (300), and cheth

(8), and there you are. 666. You can do it other ways, too. Try using the Chaldean system or the Pythagorean system. Same results."

You're feeling a bit overwhelmed. This wasn't how you expected Judgment Day to be. You try to explain.

"Well, of course we're glad to see you. Maybe we'll get used to you. But did you ever think maybe you're asking too much of us. We didn't think you'd be a nasty old drunk and a slut."

Jesus looks at his outfit in surprise.

"Well, to be honest, there seem to be so many old drunks around on the streets, I thought that was a model you liked. These are not exactly to my taste, but since this is what you supplied, I, of course, thought they were your best things you were offering to clothe the naked, as per my instructions. I didn't want to hurt your feelings, especially at a time like this."

He thought for a while, jiggling a sandal on his toe.

"Okay, here's a thought. I was trying to appear in a form that I thought you had indicated for me. After all, that's what Judgment Day is all about. I've been judging you for a long time, and now it's your turn. What kind of a Jesus have you shaped for yourselves all this time I've been away? I left it all in your hands.

"Let's make it simple. Just this. Who do you say I am? You tell me, I'll try to be whatever you say, and we'll take it from there."

Hurried little consultations begin.

Well, I always pictured him as taller than usual, but not so tall as to be freaky. How about six-four. No, that's a little too much. Six-two. Hair should be a little long even if it's not the style. But we don't want him looking like a sixties wannabee. How about just a little long, sort of like that new age singer Yanni? That's good. Light brown with golden highlights, can we agree on that? A little wavy. You've got to go wavy if you go long. Otherwise you just look unkempt.

The leaders of the church are powerful and for a while their thoughts prevail. Soon a sanitized, updated version of Holman Hunt's painting stands before them, dressed in pleated Dockers and a nice soft shirt, flannel but with a tiny houndstooth check that's a little dressy, from L.L. Bean. At the last minute, they add, not really a halo, just a hint of highlighting all around his head. He's got Boatsider moccasins on his feet and the gold strappy sandals look sort of forlorn, kicked over in a corner, one standing up and the other fallen on its side.

During Jesus' time in the downstairs bathroom, the teen-age youth group has come in and been motioned to the back of the room. They missed the scruffy Jesus but giggled with joy at Jesus in drag. Being young, their thoughts don't have so much authority, but they've used their cellies to text one an-other and now they're all there, so making up in numbers what they might lack in age.

They don't like their parents' preppy Jesus at all, so they continue to punch in their thoughts about Jesus, and as each message shows up on their screens, Jesus changes accordingly.

Soon he is a five-foot eight-inch dirty blonde with a shy smile, wearing a Weed Is For Prophets T-shirt, torn jeans and rubber flip-flops, so homey that one of the Youth Group skateboards right across the room and high fives with him, totally ignoring whoever yells at him from across the room to go back to his seat how dare he and they'll have something to talk about when they get home.

After that, things go back and forth for a while. Six-feet-two but with dirty blond hair and flip-flops. Executive wingtips, five-feet-eight wearing a T-shirt. And so on. However, word has got around, and the church is full. By the time the vegetarian People for the Ethical Treatment of Animals group has him in undyed cotton trousers with a drawstring and a natural linen shirt with buttons carved by Fair Trade craftspeople, with definite cocker spaniel eyes, everyone is tired and asks for a break.

During the break, you join the smokers in the vestibule. The temperature has dropped quite a bit, and the wind is starting to whistle around the corners. You've kept your indignation bottled up inside and welcome the chance to vent a little.

You say this is not what you expected at all. You don't think it's quite fair. It's asking too much of you. After all that authoritarian stuff, the Ten Commandments and the Sermon on the Mount, to throw it all on your shoulders! You tell people confidentially that you don't know if you've ever mentioned it to anyone, but you tithe. After taxes of course.

Although indignation is rising, you're all still afraid of overt rebellion. You go back to the hall and take your places. Things have been continuing in your absence. Jesus is patiently waiting there, now with dreadlocks, overlong hip-hop shorts and a size quadruple-X, super-extra-large white t-shirt. He must have got tired of coffee, so someone has seen to it that he has a bottle of water.

You look at him and think what a shame all this is. He was at his best when he was just a little kid. It was a lot simpler. Surrounded by all that Christmas stuff, his mom and dad nearby, shepherds and lots of animals, angels singing in the sky. All of a sudden, you think, that's who I think you are, Jesus. You're Baby Jesus. That's the Jesus we all loved best.

Immediate result. You watch the clothes falling to the floor as the figure transforms backward. Young man Jesus to teenager Jesus to Baby Jesus on the floor, cooing and gurgling. Definitely a golden glow around his head.

Tension magically seems to leave the room. You all let out a sigh of relief. This is more like it. This is a Jesus we can relate to. Everybody walks up quietly, towering over Jesus, looking down at Jesus.

Secretly, you all think it would be good if he just stayed like that, a cuddly little no-problems baby. Then, unbidden, a thought creeps in. Life was pretty nice for most people before he even came. Maybe it would have been better if he hadn't even been baby Jesus, just had never been born.

Leave it for sometime in the future, all this theology. It's hard enough just getting through life, going to work everyday, making a nice life for your family. It would be good if the Second Coming, hell, even the First Coming, was just something on the agenda for way, way in the future.

Jesus, well, as soon as you think that, Jesus down there on the floor seems to be having some breathing difficulty. As you watch, the little figure sighs, grows paler and paler, seems to curl in on himself. As you watch, he becomes ever smaller, less defined, finally a little fishlike creature, then a blob, and finally a few cells that dwindle on the floor and disappear.

You feel really scared while this is happening. You didn't mean to go that far. Have you killed Jesus? Wait, you say, but as soon as that comes out of your mouth, you forget what you were going to say next.

You all stand around blinking and looking a little dazed, stretch as if you're waking from a dream. Nobody remembers who the speaker has been, and nobody wants to embarrass himself or herself by asking. Guest speakers are like that. Improving and all, but sometimes you just have to let the words flow over you and doze a little. It's been a very nice get-together, you say, and agree to do it again soon. People gather up their casseroles, wipe off the table, and stack the used plates and cups in the dishwasher.

As you go out, something seems different, empty. That's it. That big empty space by the door, nail on the wall. What used to hang there? Must have been up a long time—that funny cross-shaped space is darker than the rest of the paint. You can't remember but agree it would be a nice spot for a painting or something, or else you should get the sexton to take the nail down. You hurry to gather up your things and start on the way home before darkness sets in.

Your armored vehicles are waiting outside to take you home, but first you all put on body armor and strap on your sidearms, put on your breathing masks, before you leave the building. You can never tell about a breakdown. Word has it the hordes of Genghis Khan and the Storm Troopers have wiped each other out, but there's always some crazy new group coming along.

Calling goodbyes, you leave the hall and step into the light of the lurid lime-green sunset, a little laboriously sucking in filtered air from the poisonous atmosphere. It's hard even to stay upright and walk in the non-stop, whistling, icy blast of wind. The heavy black snow is coming down harder now, and the wolfish things are howling in the distance.

First Life

WHAT CAN I SAY?

I was young.

I remember hearing my parents talking to some guests one time when they were entertaining.

"God has such an interest in those little humans he invented, and I have to admit they're really cute—just like us, you know, except tiny. He's built a whole world for them up there in the attic, like a gerbil run, but much much more complex. Oh, you'll have to see it to believe it. When are you going to let us come up for the grand tour, honey?"

I smiled and said sure, anytime, right now if you want. But I knew they weren't going to walk up those narrow wooden stairs, so splintery and dusty, and when they turned back to the company and offered them another drink, nobody even saw me slip away.

Eden, the old family home. It's pretty much gone now. I've spent the last few centuries clearing out the house, seeing if there's anything worth saving. Sure it's depressing, but it's got to be done. The whole place is dangerous, collapsing under its own weight.

Just a couple of days ago, I came across this—my so-called lab notebook. Would you believe it? Been up there all this time. Those smeary places, they're mostly chocolate, but, hey, I'll admit it, a little blood. Reading it's scary, quite frankly. Typical kid stuff mixed in with scientific jargon I picked up in *Popular*

Science magazine, the Bible of my childhood. Read it cover to cover. Found a bunch of them up there, too.

But what I was doing in those days was, to put it bluntly, practicing torture. My little humans died from my experiments. Once I drowned a whole bunch of them to see what lengths they'd go to trying to crowd on one little boat I'd had them build. Encouraged them to slaughter one another. Rained fire down on their little homes. Nobody even noticed. I just wrapped them up in newspaper and out they went with the garbage.

One of my rules, I called them my protocols, was to get the little creatures to do everything themselves, so one day I put a particularly sleek little beast I called Gloria in a breeding box with a handsome young male and let nature take its course.

After I was sure she was pregnant, I put the young male in one of my towns—I'd modeled it on the wild west stories I was crazy about—way over on the other side of the attic. I remember picking him up like a kitten, kicking and struggling, but he settled down pretty fast when he saw the muscle cars and beer I'd stocked the place with.

As for teenage Gloria, I had her look for an abortion in a storefront clinic in the shabby part of her little town, where late at night the off-duty person did what had to be done, stabbed at her a few times, pocketed her cash and sent her home. The future David Kennedy Brown was still cozy in his warm nest, undamaged except for the tiniest bit of brain. I was getting a little more sophisticated in my experiments.

"Right on target, bingo," I remember thinking and wrote it down in the notebook. Right here, see?

"The male wasn't important so I got rid of him and fixed the female just right."

My parents were, I would say, kind, in the way people of their generation were kind. They wanted to raise me right, helped me remember to feed the cat. Taught me to rescue house spiders by putting a glass over them and sliding a piece of paper under so I could take them outside. Problem was, I didn't get any moral direction. I had to figure everything out by myself. At meals, they'd ask me about what I was doing, and I'd tell them totally misleading stories, and they'd smile at me and be content.

They didn't have a clue about young David Brown's painful life, all documented here in the black-and-white notebook. Those blobs on the page, those are the tears I shed last night when I was reading this horror story. I read this, and I am appalled, have no idea how I became the god I am now—human rights advocate, a god for the poor, the abandoned, the abused. A god of love and compassion. But I had to grow up with no help from anybody, and along the way I caused a lot of damage.

Poor David, I think as I read this. He never had a chance. Why didn't anybody ever look at what I was doing and straighten me out?

They just left me all alone with my attic world full of little humans. Including poor David. I created him to be on the borderline, to see what he would do. Too slow to keep up, smart enough to realize nobody wanted him. Not even his mother. That was understandable, of course. Small towns in those days were not kind to unwed mothers. She spent a lot of her time praying aloud, to *me*, to be forgiven for the sinfulness, as she saw it, that she totally blamed herself for. She'd long since forgotten those nights of hot wind and warm hands with the young man I took away from her without a word of explanation and banished over on the far side of the attic.

To tell the truth, I'd never paid much attention to her. She just kind of wandered around like a lost soul for a while, and then she found some friends in a little group that called itself the Baptized Apostolic Church of Repentance. The poor little beasts liked to use fancy language to describe their institutions and ceremonies.

On one occasion I picked up a prayer she was saying on her knees thanking God All Powerful (she meant me) for sending David to her as a reminder against temptation. Somehow my little humans had developed the idea that everything that happened to them was part of a grand scheme, all planned out ahead of time for some wonderful reason known to me alone.

At the time, I remember thinking I had been a little rough on her, and I was glad she was happy about it all because I could see she had changed from the sleek, laughing little beast she had been before.

It seems so far away, so long ago. The little towns in the attic are pretty much fallen into splinters, and the sun and moon, the stars, all ran down long ago, and they've crashed down on the floor. After I left home, the little things somehow left the house, crawled down the ivy, I suppose, and spread all over. Several billion of them now. I do the best I can to keep an eye on them, but they're a rowdy, quarrelsome bunch.

A while back I invented souls to make it all up to them. When they die, I revive them and put them in a very nice fourth-dimension sort of place I've fixed up, greenery, plenty of food and water and nesting boxes. Heaven, I call it. They're still worth watching, invent things, think. Their ideas about me continue to evolve, interestingly coming closer and closer to the god I really am now, but I can't get over all that suffering along the way, when they were imitating me as I once was.

Well, to make a long story sort of medium, and I thank you for letting me get this stuff off my chest (thanks, just a splash), I set it all up and then just watched, taking notes on what was happening and what they were thinking. You sure you want to hear all this?

Gloria, well, in her mind she has nothing to reproach herself with, insofar as taking care of David. She's a good mother, feeds him as well as she can on the pay of a night-shift waitress and keeps him clean and neatly dressed.

She doesn't remember how easily she once lavished kisses and caresses, so the stiff, dutiful care she gives him seems as good to her as any other kind. She knows he isn't happy, but since she doesn't believe that happiness, vaguely sinful, is desirable, she tries to train that expectation out of him.

When he reaches the age of lustful temptation, as she thinks of it, when she got in trouble, she disapprovingly accepts the 6-pack he consumes every night because it keeps him passive, groggy, at home, out of trouble. Every night he sits unseeing in front of the television, steadily sipping for his newfound forgetful dreaming, retreating from his lack of love.

See, the problem with David is, he tries. He knows he tries, but nobody likes him. Maybe he understands a bit about his mother, but he works hard at his job, one of the best workers there, and even the boss doesn't like him. He thinks they all know he doesn't belong there because he isn't as slow as the others, thinks they're jealous, that's all. I wrote it down, all his pain. It existed so I could write it down in the notebook.

He thinks even though he was in slow classes, he's gone to regular high school. He looks nice. On the street, regular girls look at him, and he would talk to one of them sometimes if he knew she was just average, not super-smart or something like that.

He hates being alone all the time, going on his break all by himself. He thinks he's lucky he can read, but even a book with good pictures isn't like talking and joking around with the others. They show their dislike of him in many ways. For example, if one of them has a sniffle, everybody says, "Go take an aspirin, lie down in the lounge for a while." Then at five o'clock, the boss says, "If you feel like this tomorrow, stay home." But they ignore him. If he stays home to get better, when he gets back, they act as if he's been faking.

Even I started to feel sorry for him, but I had to write the progress of the experiment down in the book and somehow, maybe because they were so much smaller than I, it was hard to think they had feelings that mattered. Do you worry about swatting a fly?

So he learns the art of camouflage. When there are parties for the workshop group, he always goes, thinking maybe this time he'll dance and find some buddies, but it never happens, of course.

It isn't planned that way in the notebook.

So he stands around and tries to look relaxed, but everybody knows he's miserable and nobody cares. Sometimes he fills up two paper cups with soda so it looks like he's holding a drink for someone who has gone to the bathroom. Of course it's so he doesn't have to go back to the kitchen for a refill so often. When he goes there, they stop talking, and he can hear them thinking at him LEAVELEAVELEAVE until the force of their dislike pushes him out, as helpless as the cork in a champagne bottle. When he's gone, the voices explode into laughter behind him.

In short, he's rejected by everybody, the normal and the abnormal, because he is in-between. Nobody wants him, he doesn't fit in anywhere, and he is smart enough to know it, so he succumbs very easily to the next step.

Remember, I was just a kid. If the swirling dreams I began to send to desolate, beer-sodden David night after night, leading him insidiously back, back through his life are vague and cruel, it is only because the little attic experimenters are often careless about their hypotheses when faced with the absorption of lab work.

Back to high school. Remembered as crisp, cool autumn, walking to school in the right heavy sweater Mom has chosen and the right faded jeans. Then comes the full impact of the tolerated reality after that crisp walk to school, and so pretty soon he is glad when junior high comes, but he sits in the cafeteria for a night, near others who talk and giggle while he pretends to be absorbed in a motorcycle magazine.

In the second grade, no one will paste with him until finally the teacher, a nice girl, says she will be his partner, and he dumbly pastes with her and goes home to Mom and church about Hell that night.

Crawling on a cold linoleum floor another night, he sobs in lonely pain when someone steps on his fingers.

"David! Stop crying! Why are you always so much trouble?"

He goes back chronologically for a long time because I knew from *Popular Science* that regression was dangerous and had to be done gradually. But after many nights of dreaming and crying out in his sleep and going to the refrigerator to gulp down beers and back into cold, grey sleep, poor little David never finds one place, one time, when he has been wanted.

Oh, yes, back, back many nights in his little crib, drinking milk from a glass bottle propped on a cushion until finally one night he is born into a terribly cold, bright world while she screams at him in hatred and thrusts him out of her arms so violently it's lucky the nurse is standing so close.

The next day, after that dream, he doesn't go to work and stays under his blanket all day, hardly moving. Ah, but that night he sleeps so happily, and for several nights and in the days he whistles at work and at night drinks his beer quickly, so he can spend more hours in the warm time, the safe time.

But this is the part that keeps me from sleeping at night. The plan, as written, was to let him re-live and realize all the way to the beginning. Imagine this.

He knows he is in the safe interior of his mother. It's warm and cozy, dim darkness, the comforting beat of her heart always near him. In the beginning, maybe, it's a little too snug with his arms and legs all wrapped around himself, but he grows smaller and smaller until he is like an astronaut floating at the end of his life support system. He is finally happy. He is safe at home, swirling and diving and tumbling in the amniotic fluid.

Then I had to stop his heart quick before the screaming woke up my parents, and now I can't sleep, and think where will I find mercy for my own soul, but at the time, all I thought was . . . no, wait . . . here, let me read you what I wrote down in my bloody black-and-white notebook:

"The experiment has been really interesting. When David felt that long sharp instrument stabbing at him . . . wow!"

The Apostle Diaries

I. Philip Meets the Ethiopian Eunuch
on the Road to Gaza

Acts of the Apostles, 8:25–40

Here's Philip waking up one morning thinking he'll have a reasonably easy day. He's combing his beard when that telltale shimmering of the air and that giveaway pre-vibration of the surrounding molecules alert him to a message coming through.

He braces himself, and then the no-nonsense voice of God tells him he has to leave Jerusalem, where he has been meaning to have a cheap, leisurely lunch at a little cafe the tourists haven't yet discovered, sit a while in a cool garden munching a fig or two, and mull over events in the tumultuous first century Christian community.

Now, as so often happened when dealing with God, a complete change of agenda. Only time to grab a quick bite before he gets on the road to Gaza, and alas, there's nothing in the house but some stale bread and half a cup of sour wine; nevertheless, he starts out with a stout heart, wishing God had let him know this last night so he could have got an early start in the coolness. Why does it have to be ungodly to plan ahead a little?

Two hours into his journey, the sun is up strong, and his sandal strap has broken so he has to carry them and go barefoot on the rocky, dusty road, and he kind of wishes Jesus hadn't made that rule about disciples not taking any extras with them when they went out proselytizing. If you're not thinking about luxury, would it be so bad to take an second pair of sandals and a nutritious, inexpensive snack?

In quite another part of the city, roads are preparing to cross. Queen Candace's Ethiopian Eunuch has also been dispatched to Gaza to interview a new candidate for the harem. He has woken up late and throws on whatever robes he can find, settles his turban, and scrabbles through the litter on his table to find something to read in the chariot.

He grabs a scroll, thinking it's that action-adventure one he was reading the night before about the hideous end of a slave trader who specializes in kidnapping and eunuch-izing young boys, runs out to the Queen's stable, his slippers going clop-clop-clop, and discovers to his irritation that, far from getting a gilded chariot with a prancing young steed, he's been assigned a dingy cart pulled by a donkey. Nevertheless, he grabs the picnic basket his young servant brings him and sets out on the road to Gaza.

Philip has been trudging in the dust for three hours when the chariot catches up with him. The donkey is ambling along but his speed still beats walking. The Ethiopian Eunuch is bored to death with the scroll he's been reading in a sort of desultory way (it turned out to be the Prophet Isaiah). Philip is tired and thirsty. It's a match made in heaven.

The bored eunuch thinks Philip looks like a trustworthy sort of fellow and asks him if he'd like a lift. Philip thinks the eunuch looks a little flashy—that pink and green turban—but he sees the scroll and thinks he's probably an educated sort, so he accepts. They shake hands and share personal histories.

Philip, knowing Jesus' followers are still seen as fringe elements by a lot of establishment folks, is nevertheless up front about his affiliation and says he's an advance man for the new Christian movement. Ali shows his superb sophistication, stemming from a lifetime at court, and says his niece in Corinth is terribly interested in Jesus and has written how much she's looking forward to a lecture by Philip's colleague, Paul.

Philip feels a little shy when Ali, as we will call him to avoid saying the Ethiopian Eunuch every time, tells him his job, but he gamely asks, "Well, how are things in the eunuch business these days?"

Ali, realizing it's pretty safe to be honest with someone not of your own class whom you'll never see again, pours out his heart about how hard it is never to have a hope of a sweet little wife and children and a rose-covered cottage, the awful intrigues of the palace, and so on.

Philip is nodding off, but he knows the code of the road: the one getting the lift has to provide some entertainment for the one offering the lift, so he forces himself to brighten up and ask some interested questions. When Ali starts to cry, Philip tries to distract him by saying, "What are you reading?"

Ali says, "Oh, it's this Isaiah thing. Someone trying to get me to introduce them to the Queen sent it as a bribe, but I can't make heads nor tails of it. It's terribly depressing and full of all sorts of metaphors and tropes and meter, even stanzas. The author might as well give up and go into copying the classics. This stuff is never going to catch on. It's a load of poetic codswallop, if you ask me."

"Why, I know Isaiah very well," cries Philip. "Really, if you understand what's going on, it's awfully good. Here, let me read it to you and provide a little *explication du texte* as I go along."

Well, this offer is irresistible. There are few things as enlivening as being one of the few people to understand a new literary find, and Ali succumbs to the temptation of being able to talk knowledgeably about an author so obscure as to be incomprehensible to the casual reader. He perks up considerably as he has a vision of himself at one of Queen Candace's little poetry afternoons, defined by knowledge rather than anatomy for a change. He falls all over himself accepting.

As Philip reads and explains, Ali grows more and more animated. You can just see he's going to become an Isaiah-bore and tell everyone he meets from now on about this marvelous new author. He grabs the scroll from Philip and begins to read, giving Philip a chance to catch forty winks. Philip has just nodded off in a nice restorative nap when the Ethiopian Eunuch shakes him awake, and the donkey cart jolts to a stop.

"What-what-what?" stammers Philip, looking around in amazement and wondering where he is.

"Look!" says Ali. "We're right beside a splendid little river!"

"So?" says Philip.

"So, what's to stop me from being baptized right here and now, just as you were explaining to me."

To make a long story short, that's what they do. Philip dunks Ali under the requisite three times and Ali, greatly refreshed, tells his servant to hand down the picnic basket, and they prepare to celebrate Ali's new life.

Unfortunately, just at that moment, right when Philip is reaching out for a crusty roll and an aromatic dried fish, God, probably impatient with the literary loitering that is beguiling his designated disciple, snatches him away in a whirlwind. The great saint, holding down his robe with one hand and his beard with the other, gazing regretfully at the picnic basket, is above Ali's head in the wink of an eye, just like Dorothy and Toto being whisked out of Kansas.

Ali shouts after him, "Write. A letter will always reach me at Chief Eunuch, care of Queen Candace. We'll do lunch!"

He waves after Philip. Philip tumbles head over heels and grows smaller and smaller as the whirlwind whisks him off to Gaza, but the Ethiopian Eunuch knows he counts now and his life will have more meaning than palace intrigue, new additions to the harem, and the latest shades of pink and green for his turbans. From now on, he's going to be a literary arbiter in the court and, who knows, might have the courage finally to publish to acclaim the slim volume of graceful poems he's been working on for the past several years.

II. The Ethiopian Eunuch's Niece Priscilla Meets Paul and Timothy in Corinth

Dear Uncle Ali, Well, it's nice to think you had such a pleasant experience with Philip, but I have to tell you that not only was Paul a disappointment, he set the cause of women's rights here back *millennia*, and although I'm mature enough to deal with the man's misogyny, I had taken my two friends Cleo and Melisande, who, believe me, weren't terribly happy to leave off voguing and strutting at the Temple to Aphrodite where they would undoubtedly have met some good-looking boys and done their duty for the goddess without any commitment, but they dressed up nicely for the lecture (braided their hair and wore some nice *faux* gold and pearls) so they wouldn't be left out when everybody was talking about Paul because, believe me, you may say it's wild and wicked Corinth, but not enough happens here that a new movement, even represented by someone as short, bandy-legged, and hook-nosed as Paul, is going to be missed.

However, I have to say the man couldn't hold his liquor, and when the crowd started arguing with him, he ended up on the floor. His roadie Timothy, who is as delicate as Paul is rough, fielded all the questions for his boss and basically told all the women present they shouldn't speak up even to their husbands and should never under any circumstances be allowed to speak in church, so you can imagine that as far as it goes with us girls, we're staying away from Christians from now on and thinking the Temple to Aphrodite is looking better and better, even if you have to climb all the way up to the Acrocorinth, since we can wear something nice, chat a bit, and unlike Paul's little gathering, it's a nice dark place where you can dally with a stranger and not have him shaving in your bathroom the next morning. Dear Uncle Ali, I'd love to write more but I have tickets to the Isthmian games, and I'm dying to know who's going to win the literary contest and get that crown of wild celery. So I'll say bye-bye for now, hoping to see you soon!

Love, Prissy

III. *Two Thousand Years Later, On the Road with a Philip, a Paul, and a Prissy*

Three hundred miles outside Salt Lake City, rain pouring down like beer from a busted barrel, I was standing beside my broken-down old junker with my thumb out, thanking God I didn't waste money on getting the doors painted to match the rest of it. I was going to abandon it beside the road, and nobody was going to come looking for the owner of a heap like that. Besides, with any luck at all, by the time anybody paid any attention to it, I'd be out of reach of the Mormon police.

I'd put all the worldly goods I cared to keep in my backpack, not meaning ever to come back. Two pairs of pants, three shirts, some underwear, my razor and toothbrush, the *Norton Anthology of Poetry*, and my collected works. My only luxury was my laptop and my 4G mobile wifi. I could economize on anything but that.

I knew if I didn't get to this event in Tucson at the Medusa Bar, I'd never get another booking with this particular Performance Poetry Speakers' Bureau, and I knew I didn't have a ghost of a chance to make it. It would have to be this gig where my car failed. The Medusa had promised recording equipment that would end in my first CD, the one that was going to let me spread my poems all over the country and free me from the insurance game. Now damn Fate wasn't going to let me make it.

Took the last swig from my pocket flask and turned up the collar of my trench coat. Didn't really give much of a damn. There's always another Medusa Bar, and Performance Poetry Artists of my caliber aren't a dime a dozen. Quarter a dozen, maybe, but there's always someplace that'll let you recite for a beer and a hamburger, usually even spend the night on a broken sofa somewhere in the back.

Wasn't a main road and it was late. I was just about to start trudging down the highway when I saw a car slowing down, but even in the pouring rain with smoke coming out from under the hood of my ex-car, I took my time to check them out. Too many weirdos. Didn't want to end up tied down with duct tape while some twenty-first-century Thomas De Quincey on uncut opium tattooed my whole body with Baudelaire.

Guy driving was older, thin hair, big nose, worn leather jacket, looked like he was nursing some secret sorrow. Still, I had a good feeling about him. He looked like he would take on responsibility for the whole world if you asked him to. Big sad eyes like a cocker spaniel.

He leaned out. "Havin' trouble, bud?"

I explained the problem, asked if I could bum a ride.

"Sure thing, bud, jump in," he said. The front seat was full of gorgeous blonde arm candy so I got in the back and pushed all the boxes of paper and books over.

I explained my name was Philip and he said, "Sure thing, bud. I'm Paul and this's Prissy."

I still wasn't too sure about them and kept my keys in my hand, all the keys sticking out from between my fingers, like I'd seen on a ladies' self-defense program on TV, taught by an ex-cop.

The whole car reeked of cigarettes. That habit his generation has so much trouble with, a weakness of the flesh that just goes on and on. Still, with his daughter, pretty blonde with lots of hair braided and looped and enough gold it had to be fake (for sure with an old car like this), the next few miles could be interesting.

We drove along for a while, and I'll be damned if the car didn't start to buck and stall. Paul pumped the gas vigorously and it started up, went a few more yards, coughed and stopped dead. Rain was still coming down. Nothing in sight except the motel we were practically in front of, one of those that was a dozen little cabins scattered in a field and a neon sign that kept flashing on and off in blue and red with one missing letter (of course). Prissy was putting on some lipstick and combing her hair in the little mirror on the back of the sun visor.

Nobody said anything for some time. Finally Paul spoke up.

"We're not going anywhere until morning. Maybe this rain'll stop, and I can get a look under the hood."

I didn't feel it was my place to offer suggestions.

When Prissy spoke up, I suddenly had all my misgivings back.

"Do you think it's safe to stop here? Are we far enough from the city?"

Oh, great, I figured. Bank robbers on the run.

"Not much choice. I've got enough we can stop here for a night, I reckon. What about you, bud? Got any money for a room?"

"Not and eat, too. I wasn't planning on this."

"Well, I reckon we can share. I'll tell the desk clerk we're family."

"You'll find there's a sanitary cover on your toilet and drinking glass," the clerk told us proudly.

We straggled through the grass to our damp little cabin with one sagging double bed. Plastic cling wrap. I appreciated the thought.

I had a Cadbury's fruit and nut bar in my pocket, one of the big ones, so I hauled that out and offered it around. Prissy pulled some bananas and a box of those cheese crackers out of her big tote bag, and we had a pretty good meal. Then Paul got a bottle of bourbon out of his little bag. We tore the sanitary plastic wrap off the one glass provided and passed it around filled with rotgut, some hideous off-brand that had probably cost about a buck fifty a quart. The story started to come out.

We were still in the reach of the Mormons. On the edges but not beyond the reach of the Mormon mafia. Prissy was on the run and she told her story.

I had no idea, when I met Al in the Pussycat Lounge where I was working as a conversational hostess, with absolutely no funny stuff allowed, that he was one of the renegade Mormons, the ones that still practice polygamy.

See, the guy that owned the Pussycat was a big fat Japanese guy from Kyoto, Mikimoto Fujiwama, we called him Mikki, and he had the idea to make a bar in Salt Lake City like the ones in Japan, I guess, but everything was reversed for the Mormons.

Instead of the bar hostesses drinking glasses of weak tea and the customers paying a fortune for alcohol, the customers, who were Mormons, got to have glasses of non-stimulating beverages like lemonade, and they paid through the nose for us girls to have nice drinks although Mikki mixed them pretty weak to keep us going.

He charged for strong drinks and made a big joke out of how we girls could finish a bottle an evening, which we didn't, but that was what the Mormon elders got charged for. It was pretty exciting for them to see women drinking.

Well, anyway, Carl, my husband-to-be, kept coming back and always sat with me. He'd wait until my shift was over and walk me home to the single women's hotel where a lot of us girls lived. It was the kind of place where there was a kitchen for us to pop corn and make cocoa, and we'd sit in our rooms and blow dry our hair together, a nice safe place.

Nobody cared they couldn't bring guys there because most of the girls were lesbians, and I was seriously considering, after my gap year was over, vowing myself to become a Consecrated Virgin, which is a certified lay order of the Catholic Church.

But to make a long story short, I fell in love and decided not to become a Consecrated Virgin. Instead, I married Carl. He said he'd had a marriage gone wrong, but with me he knew our love was fated to be.

Boy, was I wrong. I discovered after we'd got married, and I'd vowed to God to love him forever, that he was just adding me to his harem of fourteen other wives. He'd been honest about the money, and that's how he could afford fourteen wives and already twenty-two children at the age of only thirty-eight. I didn't know then that he had a lot of . . . problems . . . and a standing internet Viagra order.

By the time I discovered all this, my virginity was a thing of the past, thanks to modern pharmaceutical companies. There wasn't anything I could do about it, and I kind of liked living in his compound. It was a lot like the girls' hotel. We wives still washed our hair together and traded clothes and had cocoa at the end of the day, unless it was somebody's turn to spend the night with Carl, which we kept track of from the schedule on the refrigerator.

When he saw I was pretty okay about everything, he told me not to tell anybody about our family (for sure I wasn't going to do that and look like a fool), and I could drive in to town whenever I wanted to get my hair done or shop. Usually two or three of us went together.

Well, that was how I met Paul, who was preaching in a little room he'd rented, and got back to my Christian roots. It was too late to be a Consecrated Virgin, but Paul said all those rules weren't important. You didn't have to be an actual physical virgin; if you had Christ, you could be a Consecrated Virgin in your heart.

Prissy leaned over and affectionately patted Paul's knee. Paul lifted his glass to her and poured himself another drink. It wasn't only cigarettes he was addicted to. Paul was honest about it—he had a major substance abuse problem that he prayed about all the time but to no avail. Prissy kept going. She knew how to tell a story.

To make a long story short, I decided to get away from the Mormons before I found myself expecting (which wasn't as likely as you might think considering fourteen wives and the way Viagra made Carl's heart beat too fast, forcing us pretty much to depend on Mother Nature). Now we're trying to put enough distance between me and the Mormons that it'll be too much trouble to come after me.

After that we watched *American Idol* on the tube and told a few jokes. At a certain point in the evening, we fell into the big bed with all our clothes on, Paul in the middle. Next day it was raining more than ever, and the desk clerk asked us how we'd liked our sanitized glass and toilet seat cover, said there wasn't a garage within twenty-five miles, but she had three old clunkers in the back yard, and we'd be welcome to any parts we needed.

"I want to get rid of those cars. My husband's long gone, and I can't afford to have them hauled. I'm just getting rid of them bit by bit and doing some good along the way."

Paul cheered up a lot when he heard that, but in the meantime, we just sat in the room and watched the rain.

After a while, he proposed that since we were both word people, me with my poetry and him with his messages, we could pass the time by reading from our works to each other.

"Fine by me. Just two people to listen," I said, "but I'm willing to give it a try."

"Wherever two or three are gathered in his name," Paul said, which sounded like some kind of a quote to me.

I read from my William Burroughs style cut-and-paste poetry and some surreal stuff I made with one of those magnetic poetry boards with little words you stick on. Paul and Prissy applauded politely but I could see they didn't understand a bit of it. That was okay. I was a writerly poet, as Roland Barthes would have said. A poet for poets.

Then Paul got out his stuff, confiding he was tired of traveling. His dream was to learn how to make a blog so he could get his message out to the world.

I didn't know what to say. Talk about a sweet guy with a great message, okay. Talk about language use, he might as well have been a Valley Girl. Like this stuff he recited off to me.

"You gotta like people. I mean really like 'em. If you don't, I don't care how good your use of language is, it ain't gonna mean nothin'. It don't matter if you know everything in the world and have fancy degrees from Harvard University, if you don't like people, it ain't gonna mean nothin'. It don't matter if you give everything you have to the poor, if you don't like people, it ain't gonna mean nothing."

He went on and on. The man had some charisma, I'll grant you that. By the time he finished swigging between every line and stopping to puff his Marlboro, the spit was flying all over the room, but you had this impression somehow that he knew what he was talking about, and you got pretty excited about it, even certified cynics like me. Put it on paper, and it was this stuff you see here. When the personal element was gone, he was a flop. He was going to be a dismal failure as a blogger.

What could I do? I rewrote for him. I may be totally into postmodern, but I reached back into my classical education and ghosted this. You'll recognize it. They practically put it on cereal boxes now. Paul's ideas maybe but my flair. One thing I always had and still do. Flair. I just took Paul's straw and turned it into gold, like this.

"If I speak in human and angelic tongues but do not have love, I am only a resounding gong or a clashing cymbal. If I have the gift of prophecy and comprehend all mysteries and all knowledge, and if I have all faith so as to move mountains but do not have love, I am nothing. If I give away everything I own, and if I hand my body over to hardship so that I may boast but do not have love, I gain nothing."

"Now that's language," I said and Prissy swooned. I'd seen her eyeing me all evening and I didn't mind a bit.

In the beginning, Paul didn't like it. Too high-falutin', he said, he wasn't trying to reach folks with fancy educations, just the common folks. I convinced him his ideas were worthy of the finest Shakespearean-type language available.

"The ideas are yours," I said, "and they're still there. I'll just spruce them up a little."

So we started there with the famous series of letters, and thanks to my wireless internet connection, I got him started with free blogging software that very evening. He had a great marketing idea, I'll say that. Every letter was supposedly sent out to a different city. We wrote one for Los Angeles, Chicago, Pittsburgh. . . . The Letters of Paul, we called the blog, and it took off like a rocket.

Now we're a mega-conglomerate. DVD's, Sunday morning national TV show, 100-voice choir with commissioned choral arrangements, our own publishing company, and all the little stuff—mugs, bumper stickers, holy dove panty hose, Christian phone cards.

One of our best-sellers came out of one night when Paul and I were having some bourbon (good stuff I bought for him and poured into a cheap bottle) outside because our own building had a no-smoking rule and Paul never had got rid of that particular thorn in his side.

I could have been a poet, I said. Paul reached over and took my hand.

"You are a poet," he said, "in the truest sense of the word. That was kid stuff, see, and now you're talkin' like a real grown-up. You had to put that kid stuff away."

It was like a light went on.

"You mean," I said, "when I was a child, I used to talk as a child, think as a child, reason as a child; when I became a man, I put aside childish things."

"You got it," he said. "Now you do somethin' with that."

I went over to the design room and gave them the new quote. It's become quite popular done in calligraphy and framed as a conversion gift.

Oh, yeah, Prissy and I got married. Paul decided he wasn't against marriage—if people thought otherwise they'd just be sleeping around—but birth control wasn't right at all, and since he still has a controlling interest in Paul's Letters, Inc., we have ten now.

Prissy's not a girl I can talk to since she became a Republican and took up horseback riding, so sometimes I say I have to work late and spend the evening at a little Japanese bar I've discovered around the corner.

Not a Mikki's. The girls drink weak tea and we're way overcharged for drinks. We pretend we don't know, the girls ooh and ahh, but I feel pretty good there.

See, it's a karaoke bar, and I'm pretty famous for singing my and Paul's words to Golden Oldies.

Judgment Day with Kelly and Michael

"Well, Kelly, the gathering here today, if day has any meaning at this point, is huge. On a dais above the crowd are the heavenly host, looking pretty much as we would expect them, given the Book of Revelation. A dazzling spectacle. The Father and the Mother, both crowned."

"I can't help noticing . . . my eyes are just drawn to the Father's long white beard. Very impressive."

"Yes, that settles a fiercely contested point, doesn't it? Just as all that wonderful religious art has showed us through the ages. The Father really is . . . a father!"

"Yes, and isn't the Mother beautiful. That outfit. Let's just take a minute and cut to our Paris correspondent, Brigitte, who can tell us all about it. Are you there, Brigitte?"

"Allo, Kelly and Michael. Eet ees a beyootifool day for ze joodgment, ees eet not? Alors, ze beautiful gown of ze Blessed Mother, or as she 'as chosen to present 'erself on such a public day, ze Blessed Teenager, will be making reverberations in ze fashion world for aeons to come."

"If there will be a fashion world."

"Zut, Kelly. Zere will *alwez* be a fashion world. *Alwez!*"

"Calm yourself, Brigitte, don't be upset. Of course there will alwez, I mean always, be a fashion world. I'd just like to point out the exquisite fabric and unexpected style of her dress. Who would have thought the Mother of Our Lord would have chosen the sixties as her decade and appeared in that shimmering white mini-skirt, a tie-dye muscle shirt and knee-high, laced granny boots?"

"Yes, Kelly, ze fabreek seems like somesing from ze uzzer world, dooz eet not, soopple and glowing as ze most expensive microfiber yet with zat mandorla effect we have seen in ze icons of ze ages, making us truly understand ze meaning of zat wonderful French proverb, *la plus ça change, la plus ça reste la même chose*, or as you say also in English, ze more sings change, ze more zey don' change at all."

"Oh, isn't that true! And so beautifully translated. Thank you, Brigitte. We can always depend on the French for just the right words for any special occasion, can't we? Don't you love her granny glasses, so bright and sparkling on that perfect little nose? They really take me back, undoubtedly a fashion statement since I'm sure she has perfect eyesight."

"And ze most outstanding fashion statement, one even a French teenager could be proud of, 'er glorious 'air! She 'as chosen to punk 'er 'air and eet ees resplendent in blond and bright fuschia, ze spikes seemingly strewn with diamonds, giving ze effect of 'er crown. So many of us remember 'er only as ze sweet young mother of Christmastide yet 'er outfit today reminds us zat she was a passionate woman when she gathered up 'er newborn in 'er arms and fled into Egypt to protect 'im from King Herod's fury."

"What do you think about those ideas, Michael?"

"I'm just waiting for a minute to get a translation of that, Kelly. Yes, I *know* she's speaking English. In many ways Mary has always been a tough little cookie, hasn't she?"

"Uh, yes, Michael, you might say that, meaning it in the nicest possible way, of course."

"Oh, of course. I had no intention of being offensive, Kelly. I just wanted to pay tribute to her strength of character."

"What a nice thought. I can't help thinking that in her kindness she is sending a special message to the baby boomer generation, who were so involved in the happenings of the sixties, both here and on the student barricades in Paris. They, including me, would certainly feel comfortable with that outfit."

"Kelly, I wonder if she appears different to different generations."

"Well, let's interview someone from a different time and see. I have here with me, ta-da, the fabulous Dame Edna! Dame, welcome to Judgment Day!"

"Thank you so much, Michael and Kelly. What a kind thought to have me here as a representative of the fabulously well-dressed older crossdresser, although many find that hard to believe."

"Well, definitely don't number me among the unbelievers. I love the way the rhinestones on your glasses echo the rhinestones on your hem."

"And on my matching panties and bra, look."

"Er, I think we'll pass on that, given the occasion . . . thank you. But what do you think of the *couture* the Blessed Teenager has chosen for the day?"

"Well, certainly not *haute*, and I did notice you'd left that part out. I've been wondering about her undergarment, with that sheer top she's wearing, given the fact that she's obviously a well-developed young thing. I would love to have an introduction to her *corsetière*."

"Michael, we're going to stop right here for a moment and come back to our guest later. The breaking news is that the Holy Spirit has just arrived and is making Herself felt by secondary effects, keeping the palms on the dais waving and providing a refreshing breeze to the crowd."

"Isn't that amazing, that even on such an awe-inspiring day, some aspects of the Trinity are thinking of the comfort of the people. Kelly, look over there. I do believe someone is coming up to Jesus."

"For those who may have just joined us, Jesus is lounging in a reassuring and informal way on the steps of the dais, wearing a simple robe but with his innate dignity, surrounded by his— may we call them—home boys, who seem to have been excluded from judgment, except for that one who is being tapped on the shoulder by an Archangel, who must be Michael, and is being sent to join the crowd below. The crowd is whispering and moving away from him. Ooooh, I think that's Judas."

"An ominous sign for those who thought all would be forgiven."

"It is indeed. Oh, look. Now a heavenly . . . presence . . . is moving toward the podium."

"How exciting! I think that's a Seraphim. Let's have a few words with our expert on angels, Professor Sees Clearly, Speaks Calmly, a Native American angelologist from Yale University, who is standing by. Professor, could you fill us in on the heavenly host?"

"Well, I could, indeed, Michael and Kelly. But may I first say how pleased I am to be here as your guest today, and I would like to make a little plug, if I may, for my new book, *I'm a Republican and My Angel's a Democrat (Guess What—It Works!)*, which is coming out from Random House sometime in the near future, that is, if we're going to have a future."

"Gee, that sounds really interesting, Professor Sees Clearly, Speaks Calmly."

"Please, call me Clem. Well, although we tend to use angel as a catch-all term, there are actually nine classes of angels, going from Angels, the least important, through Archangels, Principalities, Powers, Virtues, Dominations, Thrones, Cherubim, and Seraphim.

"And you are correct, Michael. The figure now reading the rules for Judgment Day from the scroll is a Seraph, which is the correct form, Seraphim being the plural, from the first choir in the highest triad. There are four Seraphim and they report only to God. It's not generally known but their main job is to sing creation. The world is constantly being reinvented by the Seraphim, under the direction of God, of course. For example, every new blade of grass is personally crafted by a Seraph humming his or her idiosyncratic grass song. They do have a rather fearsome appearance, as you can see, with their four heads and six wings but they are creative beings and, actually, underneath that fearsome facade, rather shy and gentle."

"Like sheep in wolves' clothing!"

"Yes, that's one way to think of them. By the way, Kelly, I thought your extremely charming fashion correspondent, was it Brigitte, might be interested in joining me for a cup of coffee to discuss the extreme makeovers these beings are addicted to, regularly shedding their wings and growing new ones."

"I don't think so, Clem. The time for hitting on women is over. Those days are *gone*. You can exit over there right now, Clem. Watch your step or not as you go down. Well, Michael, that was pretty clear, wasn't it?"

"It was, indeed. You struck a blow for women everywhere. Why should Judgment Day revive old patterns of behavior that have been legislated out of existence?"

"I mean what the Seraph explained."

"Also. Couldn't have been clearer. What beautiful diction!"

"Yes, it reminded me of those grand old stars, Olivier or Gielgud, at their best."

"It did, indeed. Well, now we understand how the proceedings will . . . proceed. One at a time, each person will present himself or herself before the dais and will be allowed all the time he or she feels necessary to present his or her case with the goal being a total review of his or her life."

"Remember, the heavenly announcer is saying, sometimes a little detail can make quite a difference. Try to present every bit of evidence you can."

"Isn't that fair!"

"Yes, time doesn't seem to be the point here. Each person can have as much as he or she wants. The point was made that if you feel you haven't explained things clearly or you have forgotten something, just tell the recording angel over there with the scroll and quill and you'll get another turn after everybody else has finished."

"I wonder just how many people are present. After all, we're going to hear from everybody that ever lived."

"Which comes to 107,000,000,000, Kelly! Worse than Times Square on New Year's Eve! But without the pickpockets, of course. We have the official method used to arrive at that number here in the press kit, as calculated by Dr. Nathan Keyfitz, who is, of course, the famous mathematician and demographer. Let me just do a brief recap of the method.

"You see, regardless of how one models $P(t)$, the population at time t, you use $P(t)$ to estimate the total number of humans that have lived in a given time period. From a time A to a later time B, the integral of $P(t)$ on [A,B] gives the total number of person-years for that time interval. If you estimate an average lifespan of twenty-five years (because remember for much of the world's history, people had much shorter lifetimes), the number of people who lived from time A to time B is approximately $1/25$ of the integral of $P(t)$ on the [A,B]."

"How interesting."

"It is indeed. Then you take as a given that exponential growth occurred in various historical time intervals [A, B], but with possibly different constants C and r for each time interval. Use C and r to match given values of $P(t)$ at A and B. This means you have to solve two equations in 2 unknowns: $P(A) = Ce^{rA}$, and $P(B) = Ce^{rB}$. By standard algebra, $P(B)/P(A) = e^{r(B-A)}$ and hence $r = \{Ln[P(B)] - Ln[P(A)]\}/(B-A)$. Once r is known, C is obtained immediately from $C = P(A)e^{-rA}$. Note that Ln is the natural logarithm, the logarithm to the base e."

"I wouldn't have thought of it that way."

"Well, that *is* the one tricky part. Then you integrate Ce^{rt} on the interval [A,B] and get the anti-derivative $(C/r)e^{rt}$ and the definite integral is the anti-derivative at B minus the anti-derivative at A. The total person-years from A to B is $(C/r)[e^{rB} - e^{rA}]$. By algebra, this is equal to $(1/r)[P(B) - P(A)]$. By substituting the value of r described just above, the total person-years from A to B is $[P(B) - P(A)](B-A)/\{Ln[P(B)] - Ln[P(A)]\}$.

"Then you apply this formula to a system of time intervals from 1,000,000 BC to the present. The sum of the total person-years for all these intervals gives the total person-years for all human life. By dividing by the average lifespan, you can get an estimate of how many people have ever lived, which comes to about 107 billion as of 2011 and then we just have to add a bit on up to the present. So we will have to listen to that many stories, and actually a few more, before we're through here. If you're interested, I'd be glad to lend you my copy of Keyfitz's book, *Applied Mathematical Demography*, although I warn you it's awfully dog-eared and underlined."

"Well, I don't think I will at this time since you've explained it so beautifully, Michael. That's a real gift I didn't know you had, to take complex scientific theory and put it in words a child could understand. Imagine, 107 billion stories. The biggest storytelling event in all time."

"There will be a few more than that since much of the world hasn't arrived here yet. Getting started has taken a few of our mortal years and all the while, people still on earth have been reproducing. But the point is, there are a lot of stories to hear."

"Yes, that angel writing it all down on a scroll with a feather is going to have writer's cramp."

"Good one, Kelly."

"It's interesting that the language here seems to be English. The press kit we were provided ahead of time noted that each person would hear the presentations in his or her native language although the speaker may be speaking something entirely different."

"Yes, Heavenish, I expect."

"Oh, Michael."

"I think something is starting. A name has been called and someone is coming through the crowd."

"It's interesting, isn't it, how many different national and period costumes there seem to be. It seems that people appear in whatever they were buried in or last wearing. What would you say about the person approaching the dais."

"That's an impressive white wig."

"Peruke, didn't they used to call them?"

"Perhaps so. From those silk (at least they look like silk) knee breeches and the long waistcoat, I don't think I'll go far wrong if I say eighteenth century."

"Yes, I'll go along with that. Oh, my, look at the buckles on those shoes. Do you think those are diamonds?"

"Let's cut to the scene. The Angel, or I think that may be a Domination, is announcing the name."

"François-Marie Arouet Voltaire."

"Voltaire. They're certainly jumping in with a high-profile personality. For the benefit of our listeners who may need to brush up their French history, Voltaire was one of the most famous figures of the eighteenth century, philosopher, wit, lover and author of the famous *Dictionnaire Philosophique*, and at the time of his death, the author of fourteen thousand known letters and over two thousand books and pamphlets."

"And I can't manage to keep up with a few dozen fan letters a day!"

"A few dozen? You're getting that many?"

"Oh, yes. Aren't you?"

"Of course. Far more than that. I was just . . . surprised . . . and happy, of course, for you. Well, no more time for personal pleasantries. Let's get back to Monsieur Voltaire, shall we?"

"I can put you in touch with my personal publicist, if you like. Oh, yes, Voltaire. I wondered if they would do that, start with someone famous, or if we would first hear from some simple, humble soul. Or maybe even a monster, like Hitler."

"They've chosen someone who was good with words, perhaps to set an example of the sort of testimony that is expected."

"Did you notice in the press kit that all souls who have ever lived, except for those finishing up a few things on earth, are gathered here today for the Judgment, regardless of where they've spent the intervening years?"

"I saw millions of yellow school buses gathered over beyond the Elysian Fields, Kelly. I expect that's how they brought the souls from Hell."

"And how about Purgatory? In the end, did it exist or not?"

"Well, let's find out from our next guest. We are fortunate to have with us here today a real expert on that subject. Let's welcome the Rat himself, né Joseph Ratzinger, better known as Pope Emeritus Benedict XVI."

"Welcome, Your Popeliness. I hope Regis' little joke didn't offend you."

"Not at all, Kelly, not at all. Actually, it made me feel quite young again. The guys in the seminary all used to call me the Rat. Then, you grow up, you become a Vatican Enforcer, all the fun is gone from life. No one ever calls you a Rat again, at least not to your face. You're a second banana until you're almost eighty. Then maybe you get to be Pope, but you're too old to enjoy it, especially since the Papal Tiara has been retired, something that was *wrong, wrong, wrong,* in my opinion. It's like getting to be Miss America, and you don't get to wear the crown. You even lose your maiden name and sometimes you wonder if the Rat is still there, under all these layers of satin and pearls."

"There, there now, Rat. Have a tissue. Here, have the whole box and share your view on Purgatory with our viewers, Rat. There, now, did that make you feel happy and young? Of course you're still the Rat, deep down inside the former Pope."

"It did, indeed, Kelly. Here, would you like an indulgence? Take two. On the subject of Purgatory, no, there isn't any Purgatory. We in the one true Church knew about advertising years before it became popular. You create the need, then you sell the remedy. People think the church runs on nothing. It doesn't. Take, for example, just these very simple pearl-embroidered velvet slippers I'm wearing. Would you believe they cost more than new seatcovers for the Popemobile? There's no off-the-rack on anything for a Pope. All custom made. People should have given freely. We had to extract every cent like pulling teeth just to pay upkeep on the Sistine Chapel. Oh, for sure. Everybody here is going straight to Hell. Believe me. I know these things."

"Well, thank you, Rat, that makes these proceedings seem pretty pointless, but maybe we'll understand more if we listen to what's going on. Don't snivel, Rat. You can continue with more of your opinions on-camera after the station break. There's a good boy. Now, returning to the proceedings, Mr. Voltaire is now standing in front of the dais, making a leg, as I think they called it in the eighteenth century, a sweeping bow, to the dignitaries, God, Mary, Jesus, the Holy Spirit. We just have to assume the Spirit is there, don't we, Michael?"

"Yes, I think we do. You can see leaves fluttering on the palms."

"It's interesting that Joseph hasn't been visible so far."

"Keeping up the same humble, low profile he's maintained all this time."

"I know, but I can't help wanting for him to get some sort of special recognition."

"Yes, he was never a flashy, show-off kind of guy. Good, steady, humble. You'd like to see him rewarded in some way. A nice plaque, perhaps. At least a certificate suitable for framing."

"Definitely."

"Look. Some sort of heavenly marshals, perhaps humble everyday Angels, are moving through the crowds."

"People are settling down on the grass. The Angels seem to be telling people to relax and get comfortable while the presentations are going on. I do believe they are offering refreshments. Can you see what they are handing out?"

"It looks like . . . could it be . . . yes, it is. A croissant-wich and a bottle of water. Amazingly, as each person takes their refreshment, the croissant-wich and water remain, reminiscent of the miracle of the loaves and fishes."

"Yes, they may be anticipating a long day."

"By the time they chew and swallow one bite, the croissant-wich is whole again. Imagine what the fast-food chains could have done with something like this! The never-ending croissant-wich."

"What I regret, Kelly, is that this wonderful invention didn't come in time to help all the starving masses on earth."

"Yes, a great deal of famine and suffering could have been prevented. When I think of those huge military transports of food. . . ."

"When all they would have needed was one croissant-wich per country. They could have passed it around."

"Well, I guess that's why he's God, and we're Michael and Kelly. These things are just beyond our understanding."

"I have something like that here in the press kit. Let me see. I know it's here somewhere. They've provided so many thoughtful things in the kit. Here it is, a direct quotation from God, beautifully needlepointed. I wonder if Martha Stewart isn't here, getting some brownie points. If you're out there, Martha, thank you! Now listen to this. Just six words but they contain a world of wisdom. *My Ways Are Not Your Ways*, in cream letters surrounded by *millefois* flowers on a burgundy background. Just put so simply and beautifully!"

"Kelly, speaking of miracles, since we've just seen the miracle of the croissant-wiches, we have here Dr. Freeman Dyson, a physicist at the Institute for Advanced Study in Princeton, N.J. Dr. Dyson, could you share with us the name of your most recent findings on the subject of miracles?"

"I'd be glad to, Michael. I recently reviewed a new volume, *Debunked*, for the *New York Review of Books*, and in the course of that review mentioned some work of John Littlewood, who was a University of Cambridge mathematician who promulgated what he called Littlewood's Law of Miracles."

"Miracles. Certainly what we're seeing today will bring that word to the mind of many of our viewers, Dr. Dyson."

"Actually, miracles are no big deal. In the course of any normal person's life, miracles happen at a rate of roughly one per month. During the time that we are awake and actively engaged in living our lives, roughly for eight hours each day, we see and hear things happening at a rate of about one per second. So the total number of events that happen to us is about thirty thousand per day, or about a million per month. With few exceptions, these events are not miracles because they are insignificant. The chance of a miracle is about one per million events. Therefore we should expect about one miracle to happen, on the average, every month. What we are seeing, the never-ending supply of bottled water and croissant-wiches, may therefore be seen as just that."

"A million happenings per month."

"Minimum."

"So to tell the story of your life, you have to cover a lot of territory."

"Let me jump in here, if you don't mind, Kelly. According to my calculations, an average person would experience nine hundred and sixty million events in an average lifetime."

"That was quick, Michael."

"Thank you. I take an interest in this. A lot of the events are humdrum. For example, drinking 21,900 cups of coffee over sixty years. Many of us have two cups. 43,800 cups of coffee. Most of those cups accompanied by words. Whomever we're drinking with. The background of news programs. Interruptions as family members ask where their clean socks are. Then all your thoughts as you drink. Oh, just in that small event of morning coffee, there's space for perhaps a mini-miracle."

"Like someone saying they love you and kissing you good-bye even though you were a bastard at the party the previous night, Michael?"

"Yes, Kelly, even that. Well, that certainly gives us some background as we begin to listen to the life story of François-Marie Arouet Voltaire. Shhhh, he's beginning and the air is, believe me, electric with tension."

"Even those who may not know who he is know what is happening and what is at stake."

"I will begin the story of my life with the first moment I drew in air. Mais non, I will begin with my conception. That two-celled organism. Yet wait, since my father's sperm and my mother's egg uniting were a link in a great chain of being, perhaps I should begin by examining what circumstances led them to their union and my existence at that particular point in time. Otherwise, I would have perhaps been quite different, made of a different egg and sperm, made different choices, not been . . . Voltaire! So, a small detour to the lives of my mother and father. And yet, they were the result of a long chain of breeding ancestors, all of whom must be analyzed, and at the time they conceived me, there were how many people on earth? I must consider the effect all these people had on one another, on my parents, and therefore on me. I must consider each moment of each hour of each day of their lives in conjunction with every event of every person who ever lived on earth."

"How long has it been since Voltaire started to present his case, Michael?"

"Well, he's reached the moment when his great-great-great-great-great-great-great-great-grandparents were conceived and he's just starting to interview all the people alive on earth up to that time and what happened in every second of their lives. He'll have to do that again for every second of his life and collate all the interactions. He also established a point about the interaction of culture and environment, so he is calling a number of scientists as expert witnesses. It will take a while."

"Including the point he made, very firmly, that he needed time to study for a few thousand university degrees to arrive at an up-to-date stance on contemporary matters in each lifetime and even what might have happened in the future, had there been a future, which he says doesn't make any difference, and write his own books on the various subjects. Only in this way does he feel he can begin to arrive at even an approximation of the reasons for his actions. All couched so beautifully in that elegant flow of language."

"His approach to his case has certainly established a gold standard for all those who also wish to avoid the other place and take their place in Heaven. "

"So each of the 107 billion plus will have to do the same. Interview every person who ever lived at every moment of their lives for every second they were alive. I personally wonder if, in the case of the inarticulate, a category of Public Defenders will arise to help them. Possibly Powers or Virtues could add this to their portfolios. Certainly the average person couldn't begin to mount such as splendid defense as we are seeing from Voltaire."

"I wouldn't be at all surprised since fairness has been such a keynote of the proceedings up to now. And a splendid defense is really a compliment to the Father, isn't it, an acknowledgement that He deserves the very best. Sh-h-h, he's going on."

"If I trace my mother's and my father's lines back to their beginnings, as I surely should, I will have to call an expert witness to the moment the first amphibians emerged from the water. Or perhaps back to that moment that air and water were separated. No, I think I must go back to the void.

"*Zut alors!* I call . . . GOD . . . to the witness stand!"

"Oh, my, that's quite a surprise, Michael. Listen to the furor from the common people on the grass. I see people fainting and, isn't this fun, a wave has started for Voltaire over there in the northeast quadrant. Listen to that cheering. Vol-taire, Vol-taire, Vol-taire. A huge surprise to the folks on the dais, too, I'll bet. I can't think anyone anticipated such audacity. And yet isn't that what Voltaire was known for? Look at that thunder and lightning."

"And the whirlwind! Our booth is shaking and the equipment, powered by I don't know what force, is flickering. I think they're discussing this shocking approach, a rather bold and definitive one, that the first defendant has made."

"Looking at it selfishly, for us, what started out as dull court reporting is exceeding OJ (remember him?) by far. This may be a good time to take a break and come back when the procedure has been established."

"Yes, I'd like to snag one of those croissant-wiches before they're all gone."

"They won't ever be, Michael. Remember? Anyway, if the defense is allowed to call God to the stand, we're going to be eating croissant-wiches for a long, long time. It might be a good time to talk about your publicist. Rat, did you get any of those little packets of mustard and ketchup? Great, would you toss a couple over here? Thanks. Ketchup, Michael?"

Why Alien Reptoids Shop
at Wal-Mart

"AMANDA, WHEN DID YOU first start to feel the aliens meant you no harm?"

"I think it was when I saw the bowls of onion dip sitting around the alien craft, Jerry. No repulsive or exotic thing that I didn't know the name of. Nothing served with an unusual utensil that I wouldn't have known how to use. Just . . . onion dip beside a bowl of chips."

"Did you have the impression this was something the aliens had put out to reassure human abductees?"

"No way. Every time one of them slithered past, out came a claw that scooped up as many chips as possible, and it would stand there feeding its face, or what passes for a face with aliens. They double dip, too. Not only did they double dip, each time they loaded so much on their chip that it overflowed on their claws."

"Truly disgusting. Did you say anything?"

"Jerry, remember I was the guest. Even if I hadn't wanted to be tractor-beamed up, I was in their home and I was brought up to know how to act in that situation.

"All I did was set a good example by taking one chip at a time, dipping just a tiny corner in an ostentatiously well-mannered way, pausing between nibbles, as one would set a good example for a kindergarten child. Then I said, slowly and clearly, 'Um, how good. No need to dip again.'"

"Were there any other types of treats?"

"Well, since we are on cable, I think I can say that while I was treated with every respect, all the male abductees were castrated."

"Castrated?"

"Yes, under sedation, then a prosthesis attached. I don't think they even noticed when they woke up. Then the aliens wrapped the testicles . . . Am I allowed to say testicle on television? I am? Okay . . . in bacon fastened with a skewer and toasted them in a little toaster oven, which I knew was from Wal-Mart because the box was still there, and set them out on a tray. Each alien took only one or two. They were more polite than about the dip, perhaps because it was a limited-supply situation."

"Did you tell the victims?"

"No, but I made a point of getting their names and addresses. One would never need to worry about birth control, unless the prostheses were better than I realize."

"Amanda, you seem remarkably cool about this experience. Was there any point at which you were scared? Were you in any way . . . interfered with . . . if you know what I mean?"

"No, Jerry. All we girl abductees had to do was sip weak tea in cocktail glasses and listen to them talk while they slurped beer and double-dipped. They had little tables set up in a corner of the craft solely for that purpose."

"What did they talk about?"

"Home. They were dreadfully lonely for their own families and all the little kiddie aliens. You have to understand that after several hours of drinking beer and speaking English through those dreadful racks of fangs and crying and carrying on, it was hard to follow what they were saying. I just said *there, there* in a soothing voice and patted them."

"So you didn't learn anything about their purpose in coming here?"

"Oh, yes, everything. They have cousin aliens here, you know, families that have been breeding with them for centuries. Queen Elizabeth. Dame Edna. George Bush. The maternal line of the Wal-Mart family. That's why the craft was full of Wal-Mart products. Obviously they get a discount. They're going to take over the world, eat all the men's testicles. . . . Oh, am I allowed to say testicle on television? I am? Okay . . . and turn the women into bar hostesses."

"So the invasion is not about tapping the earth's rich mineral resources?"

"Oh, yeah, they want the oil, too. They wouldn't have invaded us for several hundred more years if it hadn't been for the SUVs. They got alarmed about SUVs using up all the oil."

"Dame Edna?"

"She's so much more than a cross-dresser. First the women's clothes come off. Then some truly terrifying foundation garments. Then the male skin, five o'clock shadow, and an artificial beer belly. Then the full slithering glory of scales and claws. Well, you see the claws all the time under that red polish. Should be a dead giveaway."

"Amanda, why do you drop your voice when you mention the alien predilection for Wal-Mart products? Would K-Mart's Martha Stewart lines be better choices, for some unknown reason?"

"I don't know anything about that. The Wal-Mart family are part reptoid, and so they get the business. It makes sense to the aliens, I guess. Keep the money in the family. Just because you're reptoid doesn't mean you don't need money. Maybe you need more than other folks."

"How so?"

"They're obsessed with plastic surgery. The room was so crowded, some of them had to sit on the floor when Extreme Makeover was on.

"The ones that seem to be in charge—your high-ranking captains and lieutenants—are often immersed in Victoria's Secret catalogs, and the rank-and-file—your cook reptoids, your clerical workers, your clean-up crew and so on—always have Frederick's of Hollywood with them.

"These creatures are into looking good, and that takes money, especially when you have huge fat tails, waddle, you're covered with scales, have a snout, and a crocodile mouth of sharp teeth. I don't want to be unkind, Jerry, but that's how it is."

"I can't stop thinking about the . . . castrations. I guess we can't call them cannibals exactly, but did you get the sense they were interested in more human flesh? Arms and legs, I mean. Haunches. Things like that?"

"Actually, no. They only like toasted testicles. Oops, am I allowed to say testicle on television? Yes? Okay. Aside from that, they seem to be vegetarian although they do eat dairy. Eggs. Yogurt. I'm not sure about fish or chicken. All I can say is I wasn't served any while I was there.

"I introduced them to toasted cheese sandwiches, and they couldn't get enough of them. They adore buttered Pop-Tarts, especially blueberry. To be totally fair, I'm not sure they realize what they're doing when they take off the testicles. After all, they do just sort of dangle there. Maybe it's like we take the feathers off geese to stuff our pillows. In their minds, I mean.

"Actually, I think they got the idea from a Texas cookbook I saw on the craft. Prairie Oysters, it called them. From cattle, you know. They're considered a delicacy in Texas. I expect they were on the menu at the White House during the Bush years. The aliens probably thought they were trying out the local cuisine. I'm just speculating here, Jerry."

"How do they reproduce?"

"I didn't see, Jerry, nor did I ask. I'm not that sort of girl. I just wanted to be a good abductee and hope I'd get back home in time for a wedding rehearsal dinner I had obligated for months ago."

"Did you? Make it in time, I mean."

"Oh, yes. Once I explained why I was a little anxious, they were very cooperative. They excused themselves for a few hours and came back with a copy of *Brides* magazine. I explained about bachelorette parties, and they were fascinated. I wasn't always sure which of them were male and which were female, so I tried to cover all ground. Fortunately, your metromale is getting more and more interested in wedding details, so I was able to cover both sexes on attitudes toward personal grooming, professional manicures, party favors, and things like that."

"So they're interested in clothes?"

"Oh, yes. The first thing they do when you get up there is make you strip and put on a garment like a hospital gown. Then later, you see your clothes on an alien and half the time when you get them back, they're stretched. I never could wear my good cashmere sweater again. I saw it on an alien that must have weighed three hundred pounds.

"I suppose I should have been grateful I even got the right sweater back. A mother and daughter I know, who were both abducted, didn't even get their own outfits.

"'Don't you hate it,' the mother, a lovely person who runs her own beauty establishment for mature women, said to her daughter, a landscape gardener who specializes in naturalizing daffodils on major estates, 'when they return you in the wrong clothes?' Everybody agreed. I happen to know that the lost-and-found bin there is overflowing. Everybody complains about losing stuff and never getting it again."

"Everybody? You mean you get together with other abductees?"

"Oh, yes, Jerry. You see, most people think we're crazy but within the group, we find life experiences we can share. We have a weekly poker game, an evening for country line dancing, and recently our first marriage. We had the wedding in the alien craft with the head alien presiding although they had to have a civil wedding here as well."

"What was it like?"

"What, Jerry?"

"The wedding."

"It was sweet. They'd all made an effort to dress up, unfortunately mostly from Frederick's of Hollywood, but we agreed it was the thought that counted.

"They'd all chipped in and gave the happy couple a truly magnificent toaster oven from Wal-Mart. You could tell they'd wrapped it themselves by all the claw tears in the paper. They'd even made a wedding reception, with bowls of chips and onion dip and buttered Pop-Tarts. Huge bottles of Mumm champagne. Lots of onesies and other baby gifts. They'd got different kinds of showers mixed up, and the bride *was* a teensy bit pregnant. One of those cultural misunderstandings you hear so much about."

"No uh . . ."

"Toasted testicles? Oh, I forgot. Did you say I could say testicle on television? I can? Okay. No, at least not in plain sight. There *was* a bacon smell in the air, and they'd come out of the back room munching, but we girls resolutely avoided the subject and, as I told you before, the guys didn't have a clue.

"After the party, they tractor-beamed the guests down first, and then the happy couple came down looking just like the bride and groom on a wedding cake. She tossed her corsage about halfway down, and a dear young girl caught it. She'd just had her first abduction experience, and the wedding was a nice introduction to this new lifestyle for her."

"Are you married, Amanda?"

"I'm happy to say I am, Jerry. Five years this June and the proud mother of three-year-old Joshua."

"How does your husband feel about all this?"

"Jerry, although we're only people of modest circumstances, we decided to have a pre-nup, so we agreed before we got married that we could keep on with our own activities. I explained to him about my obligation to spend some time as an abductee, but he said he thought I was just a great little kidder. Then he saw me returned in mid-air, dropped down on our bed from about three feet up, and he freaked. Usually my landing is much better. After that, we went through a period when he was jealous, and we had to go for counseling. He even insisted on DNA testing to be sure Joshua was his."

"Would he like to be abducted, too? So you can share this experience?"

"I explained about the toaster ovens. He dropped the subject right away."

"Well, Amanda, on that note, I think we'll have to leave you. Thank you for sharing your experiences. I hope you'll come back again and share more details of your fascinating life with aliens."

"I'd be pleased and proud to do so, Jerry. Thank you for having me."

Modems to Hell

JUDGMENT DAY, after a restless night of sweat-drenched sheets. Six-forty-five, and they finally got up. They decided not to go to work, but the thought of not going nagged. The Dean had said they must make up their own minds, and the purges of the new administration were still going on. It was a Hobson's choice. If the world didn't come to an end, they might well lose their jobs.

"Do you realize," Alison said, "that the idea of losing our jobs is so ominous that we're rooting for the end of the world?"

It had come on too suddenly for people like them. She thought bitterly of the disadvantages of affluence and education. The inhabitants of the West Virginia hills and the crazies in California had had time to repent, clean up their acts, get rid of possessions. They had undoubtedly heeded the thunderous announcements and writing in the sky. They had leaders to herd them to hilltops and simple frame churches while people like themselves smiled and joked until it was too late.

"I think I'll go up to the mini-market and see if there's a paper," Jean-Luc said. "Anything we need?"

"No. Well, yes. Maybe some skim milk."

"You want to come?"

"No. I'll get some coffee started. You want decaf or regular?"

"Oh, let's live it up. After all, it's Judgment Day. Make it half and half."

He drove cautiously down Poplar Avenue, noting that nobody seemed on the way to work. Was this the final erosion of the Protestant work ethic? Usually by this time, most of the cars, station wagons excepted, would be pulling out, and the street would be full of suits with attaché cases headed for the Paoli/Thorndale line. A backsliding French Catholic in this WASP neighborhood, he had expected to be among the few idling at home while the rest sturdily trudged to work to die in the saddle.

Turning left on Woodland, he passed over the creek and turned left again at the new brick power plant, noting that the landscaping was beginning to flourish. As he went past the little rowhouses with their flower-packed front yards, he wondered if the one with Jesus and his bleeding heart amidst zinnias would be singled out for special treatment.

The mini-market was closed, for the first time in his memory, but the Acme was open. The big poster in the window said "Open On Judgment Day From 6:00 To 2:00." Stepping inside the supermarket brought immediate reassurance. The food chain hadn't broken down in the face of national disaster after all, regardless of the magazine articles predicting just that—that the national food chain was always just three days from total breakdown.

As he pushed his cart along the aisles, he noted there was still plenty of stuff on the shelves but people had obviously been making inroads, just as they did when snow threatened. Whenever the radio even hinted at a few inches of snow, there was always a happy run on the supermarket.

He knew just how it went. You stopped in for milk, bread, and toilet paper. Then the desire to hibernate came on, and you added juice, and root vegetables for hearty soups, and plenty of sliced Jarlsberg for sandwiches, and some ice cream for a treat and maybe a raspberry coffee roll, and Red Zinger tea and hot chocolate for the kids. A *Weekly World News* to keep up on dwarf-tossing competitions and living two-month-old abortions with their mother's wedding rings—lost 45 years ago in the Pacific—around their waists.

Time passed as he heaped his cart, and he spent half an hour in the store, discovered when he got to the check-out that their system was down (ominous) and had to jog across the parking lot to the bank.

When he got home and saw Alison pacing back and forth on the porch, he discarded the idea of saying the phone at the supermarket wasn't working. She let the door slam in his face and didn't help carry the bags, but when she saw the food piled on the kitchen table and most of the chairs, she told him to keep her company while she put it away.

He sat at the old pine table and drank coffee while she unpacked, calling him crazy again and again as the bounty was revealed. "Raspberries! Are you crazy?" Four little cartons, filled with two-inches of designer pink globules. "At $3.89 a container?"

The riches spilled out of the brown paper cornucopias. He beamed with the complacent delight of the good provider, a cave man who brought home prodigious quantities of nuts, roots, berries, and fat young rabbits to his lovely skin-clad wife and progeny, snuggled in their warm beds of moss and leaves.

Croissants, Sara Lee cheesecake, baby vegetables, bars of Cadbury chocolate, expensive gourmet dinners—all the luxuries they bypassed weekly in favor of inexpensive, simple and nourishing fare. Soon it was tucked away in all the warm niches and chilly crevices of the cave—the cupboards, the refrigerator, the bread bin, the freezer. Far more than they could eat in a week, yet supposedly they had only this one Last Day, and it was reasonable to presume that part of it would be taken up with being judged.

Tipping heavy cream into their coffee, they greedily tucked into large hunks of cholesterol-laden coffee cake.

"I wonder if we'll have electricity all day?"

"Why not? It seems to be working okay. As a matter of fact, everything seems to be working okay. Maybe nothing's going to happen after all. Maybe it will just be like the new administration at the university. A lot of stress and worry but nothing really a lot different than it was before."

"Things are bound to change. It's just the beginning. Did you see anything happening when you were out?"

"No. Well, yes. You know the people who live three houses down?"

"The ones who walk their dogs early or late so no one will see the messes they make?"

"You've got it. The very ones. Well, he was out in broad daylight with both dogs *and* a pooper-scooper."

"Oh, you! I don't believe that."

She threw a loaf of bread at him and passed him an already melting Dove bar.

"You're just making jokes, as usual. You're too complacent. It's because you're so egocentric. You think nothing will ever dare to disturb your life. The news last night was speculating on what might happen. They advised plenty of water in case supplies were interrupted."

"What are they—survivalists? I don't think we're going to be living in our basements creeping up for a drink. This is supposed to be it—sheep and goats, the apocalypse, the four horsemen. Anyway, there's a full case of Perrier in the trunk."

"Oh, you are clever."

She leaned across the table and gave him a kiss.

"I take back what I said about your egotism. But I've been filling a lot of containers, just in case. We can use it for coffee and to wash in, if necessary. Do you think I should get the kids up early while the shower's still working?"

"Aren't they going to school?" he began to ask and became aware that the radio was on to the news station and that numbers were filling the air as they did when there was a snow-storm, signaling a day of freedom for school children. ". . . 452, 453, 454 one hour late with no transportation." They listened intently, but their school wasn't announced.

"Oh, I'll let them sleep. They can face the Last Judgment even if their hair isn't freshly shampooed."

After they had eaten three-quarters of the buttered coffee cake and drunk cup after cup of coffee in the big gold-and-white Limoges cups, Jean-Luc proposed seeing what was on television.

This was an ongoing squabble, traditional, almost cherished.

"What difference does it make? Can't you stay away from the news even on Judgment Day?"

She was capable of not answering mail for months if it looked threatening, of not answering the telephone on the hundredth ring, of sitting motionless and breathless until the door bell stopped ringing. He faced facts, opened mail promptly, and listened to the messages on the answering machine. The dance was so old and practiced as to be almost graceful, and in the end they carried their cups to the TV but left the sound down so they could monitor it in silence, remoting the volume up if anything looked important.

She had tried to be enthusiastic about the food because it was his offering, but if the truth be told, every bite and swallow was an ordeal. Deep down inside her, Calvinism lurked, and the burning fires of Hell, intellectually discarded and emotionally firmly in place, were very real and very threatening. For her. She thought there was a slim chance everyone else in the family would be okay. Jean-Luc, although brought up as a Catholic, was a firm non-believer. Sincerity was on his side.

The two kids, brought up without religion, were as innocent and safe as pagans. Only she secretly yearned for and was afraid of commitment, was ripe with guilt for things done and undone, longed for the comforting polished brass and tea urns of the Episcopalians, the simple moral uprightness of the Methodists, the Himalayan truths of Theosophy, the convenient mental healing of Christian Science. She studied them all, read the Tibetan Book of the Dead, chanted Om in bed at night, tuned in gospel preachers, then in the end retreated to Iris Murdoch and Virginia Woolf.

Surprisingly, there were newspapers, much denser than usual because of the absence of advertisements.

"I'm surprised the malls didn't think of having Judgment Day clearance sales."

"Don't be too surprised. It was double-stamp day at the Acme."

He snatched the comics page from under her hand.

"Got to see what *Doonesbury's* got to say about Judgment Day."

Doonesbury had seen them through Woodstock, Vietnam, yuppies; surely it would tell them how to get through the last day.

She began to work her way through the rest of the papers. First page. Predictable. Three-inch headlines. A dignified JUDGMENT DAY on the *Inquirer* and ELVIS TO ACCOMPANY CHRIST on the tabloid.

Stories on the announcement, which had been written in the sky and at first attributed to prankish skywriters until government jets world-wide had investigated.

A recapitulation of traditional theories about the Last Day. Speculation on the type of trumpets that would sound, written by a professor of musicology at the University of Pennsylvania, a retro-view of the earthquakes, plagues and fires that had been troublesome in the last few years, now seen to have been the traditional harbingers.

The Dow Jones had plunged, but there had been a lot of last-minute buying. Churches made their announcements, and the groups that would be expected to announce such things did indeed announce Last Judgment parties, complete with champagne.

On the editorial pages, the final results of the drive to provide dinners for the homeless on the Last Day. The results of the Take-An-Orphan-Or-Elderly-Person-Into-Your-Home-For-The-Last-Day drive.

For some reason, boxed in, the account from St. Luke of the birth of Christ but, surprisingly, nothing from Jeremiah or Revelations. As to be expected, not even a token article on the Last Day activities of the very minor minorities in the area except for a small announcement that the Reformed Synagogue would hold ongoing services all day.

"It's a bit disappointing, really. There's nothing of substance, nothing to help us know what to expect. I wish you had picked up a *New York Times*."

"It wasn't in. Maybe something has already started in New York. That's what you would expect, after all. Avant-garde judgment in New York. California won't even notice. Anyway, you have to hand it to them for getting anything at all out today."

The Metropolitan Page was pretty ordinary. Rapes, muggings, child abuse, city council meetings. Why not? The trickle-down theory had never worked, even for Reagan.

As for the television, she gave up on that pretty quickly. How many public figures could you endure being interviewed, interspersed with Charlton Heston in sandals? Jean-Luc, flipping channels with the wireless remote control, stopped briefly here and there for a last few minutes of *Leave It to Beaver, I Dream of Jeannie,* a game show, a soap. . . . They seemed so pure, so wonderfully innocent. They had never watched them, and now it seemed a lamentable lack.

"Do you suppose it will count against us?" Alison wondered. Would they receive additional punishment for snobbery, lack of humanity? After all, the saints had eschewed washing. Perhaps their steady diet of Channel 12, *Masterpiece Theatre,* the Thursday mystery had been, not cardinal sins, surely, but lesser ones, venial.

She rummaged in her book bag for a clipboard and a legal pad, rejecting fine-tip markers and biros in favor of the Waterman Jean-Luc had given her one day for a make-up present. With the edge of an inter-office manila envelope, she divided the page into four horizontal sections and drew a line down the middle. She put one of their names on each section and labeled the left section of each PRO and the right as CON. Then she began to jot down information about each of them for and against damnation.

It was difficult when you didn't have an absolute criterion to work against. Adultery, of course, but that had been in the seventies and did it balance against a faithful annual contribution to Greenpeace? She wrote both of these directly across from each other and then cancelled them with a thin line, although it could be like SATs and bad answers would be subtracted from good ones.

She sucked the pen, as she always did when pondering. She had hugged Charles when she thought he had AIDS, but it had been done in front of others, an act she had known would give her a lot of credit. The feeling had been sincere, but she had been aware of the effect. She wrote "Hugged Charles" in small, tentative letters with a question mark, instantly deducing an elegant addition to her chart of giving relative importance by the size of the letters. She could also underline and asterisk if needed.

Greed. Wasn't that one of the seven deadly sins? Should she make subcategories to each of their charts for the seven sins? Where would she find a complete list of them? Thank God she hadn't eaten more of the croissants, especially on the Last Day when it would surely count more.

As she wrote and Jean-Luc flipped channels, Lexus and Tiffany continued their blissful sleep. True, they had heard of the Last Day on television yesterday, but it, as Vietnam to their grandparents' generation, had mingled with sitcoms and commercials until all the offerings were an inseparable mingling of truth and fantasy.

Unknown to any of them, the skies were filling with angels and black trucks were beginning to rumble through the streets.

Oh, let us look at Wayne from an angels' eye view. The neighborhood is so pretty. Green, green, lush with mature trees and emerald lawns. Hosta lilies, bird baths. The charming houses date from the late 1800's and are listed in the National Historic Register. The local Finnaren and Haley store stocks paint in appropriate colors, and the Historical Society gives talks with slides on appropriate paint combinations. The houses are a mixture of standard American white with black, grey with black, cream, brown, and tan. Here and there are interspersed the green, mustard, red, blue with mauve, brown with yellow, and tangerine of the more daring members of the community.

Children, protected from knowledge of this day, are nevertheless more carefully dressed than usual in their OshKosh B'gosh overalls and beribboned hair as they play with their skateboards, bicycles, and frisbees. On several corners, scrubbed and beautiful young faces offer lemonade for the traditional price of ten cents, or, over on Walnut Avenue, a little more upscale, for as high as twenty-five. A kind thought of the parents who have helped with the small commercial endeavors.

Will the resurrected dead, long deprived of tart cool drinks, have the appropriate change? Perhaps they can reach under their tongues for Charon's coin, long put by for that first cooling sip.

But let us admit it. There are serpents in Paradise. On the corner of Radnor Street Road and Poplar Ave., two small blond children are trying out curses on others and sticking out their tongues at a passing grandmother. A little farther down, near the park, a crippled child is tormented into tears by a little boy and his sister, who call out, "flat tire, flat tire, flat tire," and swing ecstatically higher and higher as he runs and limps home.

Oh, there is much activity. Several members of the local Civic Association have gone to a nursery and can be seen unloading their station wagon near the community fir tree, where Christmas carols are sung in December, and where red, white and purple flowers grow during the patriotic days of summer. These harmless posies are pitched on a growing pile under a nearby hedge as their places are usurped by stately waxen lilies.

Many people are mowing their lawns, and two families on Woodland are painting their porches. Others are tearing out hidden pockets of dirt and clutter, clearing their basements, re-lining shelves, and stuffing black plastic garbage bags with serviceable clothing for the Purple Heart, should its trucks ever come around again. If not, possibly the risen dead will not be quite decent, and will they not be grateful for only slightly rubbed corduroys and patched Harris tweeds of professorial quality?

Dressed in stiff white shirts, ties, summer suits and spectator pumps, whole families can be seen heading toward the churches strung out along Lancaster Avenue. A work day, yes, but the services are being announced on the crawl line of the local cable company's community access channel.

Jean-Luc and Alison's house, in need of paint, one shutter awry, nestles comfortably in a bed of crabgrass. On the front porch is furniture plucked from trash piles and garage sales, paperback books stacked on the old table, a forgotten beer bottle tucked behind a peeling white pillar. Inside, they are knocking on their children's doors, bribing them awake for family togetherness with pretty breakfast trays, French toast and syrup, vegetarian bacon, zinnias in bud vases.

"It's Judgment Day, dears. We thought it would be nice if we spent it together."

Sleepy groans pointed out that Judgment Day, a day on which they hadn't been awakened for school, would best be spent in letting growing bodies have their needed sleep.

By 12:30, nothing had happened and there was a sense of anti-climax. As was their custom on weekend days and holidays, they drank innumerable cups of coffee, read, and listened to music. Not being joggers or dog-walkers, they were missing the interesting activities beginning in Wayne. Alison suggested a game of Scrabble.

"Mom, get serious! Scrabble? On Judgment Day?"

Having been serious, she became defensive.

"Do you have any better ideas? It would be nice to have family togetherness on the Last Day. I thought we could play games, and I could pop corn. We could even make fudge. It's unlikely we'll have anything like that in Hell," she concluded bitterly and immediately wished her words back.

Tiffany, however, leaped on the opportunity for speculative conversation.

"Why do you think we'll go to Hell? We haven't been so bad."

"Oh, hey, wait a minute! Let's look at things on a global scale. What about polluting the world's environment? We have sometimes been very lax about separating colored glass and aluminum cans in the recycling bins. Driving cars when we could have walked? Air conditioners! On from morning till night!"

"You've always done penance for us, Mom, by not eating poor little cows and fish."

Lexus chimed in.

"And what about the refrigerator? We always read the refrigerator and keep up-to-date on all world problems and social issues, as well as the dangers of loud iPods. You do that, Mom, no one but you!"

"On the other hand," Jean-Luc said speculatively, "what about all that broccoli she eats? I have often left the room in tears over the fate of those innocent veggies, rent into shreds by her relentless chomping teeth."

Eventually they all settled in to help fill out the PRO and CON chart, pausing occasionally, as was their wont, to squabble about fine gradations of judgment. The grids began to fill.

"Using plastic garbage bags, except at the Acme, where we ostentatiously opt for paper." On the CON side, with a PRO for making an effort, but written in very small letters.

"Contributing every year to the People for the Ethical Treatment of Animals." Definite PRO; small-letter CON for wearing leather shoes.

China, crystal, sterling silver while the homeless went hungry.

Working hard, helping the economy.

Not voting in local elections.

Folding money to bag ladies.

Taking in homesick foreign students but copying recipes on the office copier.

Running the lawnmower when the nasty neighbors were having a lawn party.

But only once.

Eventually the grid was filled, the popcorn and fudge made and consumed. They drifted off to quiet occupations. Lexus and Tiffany were playing Scrabble after all, and Jean-Luc put on some Albinoni. Curled up on the couch with the S volume of the *Encyclopaedia Britannica*, Alison was looking up the seven deadly sins when the doorbell rang. Everyone stiffened and looked at one another.

Alison let the doorbell ring several times before walking resolutely to the door. Her stomach a small cramped ball, and knowing as she had always known that no good came of responding to doorbells, she stood with her feet firmly apart, ready to make a good argument, but when she abruptly, violently threw open the door, all she was aware of was the waves of light emanating from the shining angel who smiled and beckoned, beckoned.

Hungry

QUIET. YOU SIT QUIET as a mouse in the corner. Push a little doll around and hum la-la-la so they forget you're there while they have the cocktail hour.

That's how you find out they're killing Grandma.

Not a single bite to eat or a swallow of water. Your mother is killing her mother.

That's their favorite punishment for you, too. Go to your room without any supper. They can do it to their daughter and they can do it to their mother.

You feel like a balloon somebody's lost the string of, and you're helplessly blowing in the wind.

You didn't realize they were that powerful, that they could just kill somebody, especially their own mother. You wonder if someday you'll have to kill them by not giving them anything to eat or drink, and you decide you'll never do it, never.

Dead dead dead forever, all skinny and dried out like an old sponge and nothing in her tummy. That's what Grandma will be.

Grandma that you visited in her little house of lace and cookies with real green plants hanging at all the windows and a bird feeder in the garden. Grandma who put a little bed right in her room for you when you visited so nothing could get you, and never said don't be silly when you worried about vampires under the bed, and while you were drying the dishes for her, said you didn't have to tell mommy and daddy.

Sometimes you have to be cruel to be kind. That's what they keep saying while they pour each other drinks. They're the grown-ups, and they should know. But they say everybody at your new school really likes you, they're just teasing the new kid, when you know everybody hates you to hell, and it won't ever stop until you're dead.

You know what they're telling you about Grandma is true because Mother sneaks you in, whispers something to the nurses so they look the other way, and takes you in to say goodbye so with your own eyes you see Grandma in the bed with sides like prison bars, her skinny arms that look like tissue paper with black and blue blotches all over them.

You think they'll do something, but they just stand there looking down at her, both her arms stretched out and tied down and stabbed with silver needles. Mother holds your hand in a tight grip so you can't get away.

Grandma can't say anything because of the tube in her mouth, but her eyes finally leave Mother and Daddy and roll really scared at you, like she's saying please, you'll help me, won't you? Remember what good times we had that week you stayed with me, baking cookies and sitting on the porch, filling the bird feeder? We can do that again if you'll help me.

Well, of course you start to cry, and a nurse comes running in, looking mad like teachers look when you've done something wrong. Mother shakes your arm and says shhhh but you don't care and just keep on wailing. Your father hisses at Mother that he told her this wasn't a good idea, and she hisses back at him.

Then they take you out into the hall to a little place with hard plastic chairs you keep sliding off of and say in those sweet voices they use when you fall down or get hurt that Grandma doesn't know anything anymore, it's just her old body there, she isn't hurting, is just waiting for Jesus to come and get her.

Jesus? Who's Jesus? The only time you've ever heard his name is when somebody gets mad and says *oh, Jesus Christ!*

You ask if Jesus is a doctor and will he help Grandma, and they look at each other and smile that way people do when little kids say something so stupid it's cute. How are you supposed to know about Jesus when they never told you, never let you know he's also God in Heaven and flies down like Superman to get you when you die and takes you back with him? They tell you now.

That evening they go out and stay for a long time. When they come back, they pay the hotel sitter, then ask you to sit down and tell you in their nice voices that Jesus has come and Grandma is gone.

Since you don't know what you're supposed to say, you just say okay and while you're brushing your teeth, you hear them talking about adding this to the list of stuff Dr. Samuels is supposed to help you with. Your throat and chest are bursting with pain, but for some reason you don't think you should let them know.

They take advantage of being in the city to do some shopping and hire the sitter to stay with you while they go to the funeral, that they say isn't for little girls.

At least Jesus has come for Grandma. You learned long ago that they tell you a whole bunch of lies, but that much is probably true. You sort of remember her singing, that time you got to stay with her, that she had a friend in Jesus, and if Jesus can float in air and carry people back with him like a lifesaver, he'll know about her needing a snack, and by now she'll have had time to eat several times, with Jesus.

You say you're not hungry, but they order you a fancy sandwich held together with toothpicks and ginger ale with a little paper parasol stuck in a cherry. You have to eat, darling, they say and you know you'd better do it because there's no way in the world you ever want to make them mad at you again.

The Crucifixion Party

NOW YOU HAVE TO go to school in this godforsaken hick town you live in for the sake of Daddy's career, where Mother makes a big sacrifice to live in the sticks, and the redneck children wait to ambush you in the morning, between classes, at recess, at lunch to ask why you talk so funny, and where you got your blouse, jeans, shoes, and why your mother is so skinny, and then, whatever you answer, run away giggling.

So when they ask you to the party at their church, you think maybe Mother was right, and they've just been teasing you for a while. They say you'll make cardboard crosses and color Jesus and fasten him to the cross, and then make a model of a tomb to put him in.

You don't know much about Jesus except when somebody gets mad and says *Jesus Christ*, but in this town there's a church on every corner and obviously everybody else knows about him, so you're sure as hell going to keep your mouth shut and wait to see what the others do just in case this is another trick.

It doesn't sound like a very nice party, but they say there will be cupcakes, and you're tempted by the promise of model building, which you like even more than cupcakes.

You can tell your parents don't like the sound of it, but you're pretty good at whining, and you ask until you wear them down.

"What kind of a party did you say it was, darling?"

"It's a *Jesus* party. To learn more about *Jesus*. I *told* you."

It's the cocktail hour, and if there's one thing in this godforsaken wilderness that Mother says has to be kept sacred, it's the cocktail hour. Daddy has just come home, and they're sipping drinks and nibbling from bowls of salted nuts.

"Well, I say Jesus to that," Mother says and looks at Daddy the way she does when she says something funny, and they both laugh.

"Let her go," Daddy says. "Sunday afternoon, we'll drop her off and have time for a couple of drinks and a nap."

They have a few more and give you a macaroni-and-cheese frozen dinner with weiners and apple cobbler in its own little compartment that you get to take to your room for a special treat. You can hear them in the living room over the news as their voices get sharp the way they do during the cocktail hour, but it all blurs together, and you don't pay much attention. You've heard it all before.

You want to let her go because that's the church Jim Forsythe goes to. You're ass-kissing your boss and the Janjaweed continue their mission of rape and burning. Isn't it enough we have to live in this god-forsaken town? You have to sacrifice your only child, too, when all the men who for a few short hours were thought to be alive are now known to be dead. It won't hurt her to learn something about the Judeo-Christian heritage. It's part of our culture, after all. Nobody here in the neighborhood knew there was anything wrong in that house and it won't hurt your chances for promotion, either, will it? Just don't say we have to start going to church next. The Dow and NASDAQ continue their downward spiral but I can tell you're already thinking about it. Barefoot and pregnant with the Southern Baptists is definitely not my style.

The money this job pays is definitely your style, Daddy shouts and throws his glass so it smashes, and they keep on fighting, but that's nothing new, so you look in your closet for something fancy to wear to the party.

When Sunday afternoon comes, you squeeze into the pink dress with a sash Grandma gave you for your birthday last year when you still lived near her, and lace-trimmed socks with outgrown, too-tight patent leather shoes. Since Grandma died, nobody has ever bought you such pretty things again although Mother has never let you wear the dress. You ask Mother why they don't get your clothes at K-Mart, where Grandma shopped, if they have such nice things, but Mother just laughs.

"Sweetheart, something you can play in would be better. You're not going to the opera. Maybe they'll have an Easter egg hunt. If born-again Christians have things like that. But you've really got to stop eating so many sweet things."

"NO," you thunder, and of course they let you, as you knew they would if it meant they got to have a nice free afternoon without the child to worry about.

Once you get to the party, you look around and feel satisfied, noting your dress is thinner and fluffier, your shoes more aggressively shiny than the others. Nobody else has been allowed to wear their party dress, and for a few minutes, you think that this time you will be the one who can ask, poisonously sweet, where they got their blue jeans and t-shirts, if you were that sort of person.

In the church basement, as soon as you get down the steps, you can see the pitcher of Kool-Aid and the cupcakes from the supermarket, the ones with piles of fluffy bright pink and yellow icing, the ones you admire and always want and your mother laughs at.

"Pure whipped lard, darling. No way."

The lady standing there, Pamela's mother, sees you looking at the refreshment table and waggles her finger at you.

"No cake until after the crucifixion."

Like she needs to say that out loud in front of everybody. You feel fat and stupid, like you're going to die. You think for a minute that maybe the car is still there, and you can just run out and get in. You know they're going to get you for it at school on Monday.

"She wanted to eat cake before the crucifixion," they'll say and run away giggling, making piggy oinking noises.

Damn hillbilly trailer trash. You want to kick Pamela's mother. You were just looking. She knows that. She knows you know how to behave at a party. Even if you don't know about Jesus, you would have been polite about the refreshments.

You know better than to try to explain and make things worse. You look around and think hopelessly that maybe the others haven't heard, but of course they have and are looking at you and giggling.

When the mothers aren't looking, Sue Ellen sticks out her tongue, and you make a face back as you squeeze into your place at the kindergarten table with tiny little chairs. In front of each place, there is a piece of cardboard like the back of a tablet, a jar of paste and little blunt scissors. The crayons, a shoe box of all different colors, mostly broken, the kind that spoil coloring, are in the middle of the table. Pamela's mother holds up her hand for attention.

"Good afternoon, girls."

"Good afternoon, Mrs. Averill," they chorus sweetly.

Nobody would think they're the same mean kids that like to shove people's faces down in the drinking fountain and push you out of line for the swings.

After Pamela's mother announces you're going to pray, she catches you looking around and bows her head down like a signal. You hastily put your head down after you look and see all the other kids know what to do. On Monday at recess you'll pay for that, too.

When Pamela's mother finishes reading the prayer, you get to start the party. First you cut two strips off the cardboard, a hard job with the dull baby scissors. You color the pieces brown, paste them together to make a cross and put it on the counter to dry while you color Jesus, who is naked except for a piece of cloth wrapped around his middle. You know you're a good colorer, but it's pretty boring coloring, and you have to take turns with the pink skin crayons and the brown hair crayons because there aren't enough to go around. You aren't allowed to use any color for his piece of cloth, and everybody laughs when you ask.

You think they'll paste Jesus on the cross then, but Pamela's mother announces you have to line up first. Pamela and her best friend Tiffany, the two most important girls there and the biggest show-offs in the school, go up to stand at the front of the table holding some tree branches. The rest of you have to line up two by two and lay your Jesuses down on opposite sides of the table while Pamela and Tiffany whip them with the branches.

Whipping Jesus! You think they must be doing something wrong and are going to be in big trouble, but the mothers smile at them like they're getting a school award at Open House. Pamela's mother calls it scorching like when you leave the iron on too long, and you think maybe they're going to burn up their Jesuses, but it's whipping. You know better than to ask any questions.

Then the other kids start to get out of line and horse around, so Pamela's mother gets bossy and with a smile that says I'm being patient, but you'd better settle down and *fast*, tells them to pick up their Jesuses after they're scorched and go to the stapling station and get their Jesuses stapled to the cross.

You're last in line, after runny-nose Mary, so you peer around the line and see the first two, after their Jesuses have been scorched, hand them over to Bossy Nancy and Mean Miriam, who efficiently slam staples—one, two, three—on each of the outstretched paper hands, one staple doing the job for both feet, which are just one piece of paper.

You can tell how great they all think they are as they compare their Jesuses and march around waving them and holding them up for others to see, singing in low voices they think the mothers can't hear, *my crucifixion's better than yours is*. Pamela's mom says shhhh in a very irritated voice and yanks her hand at Mary, just before you in line, to make her hurry.

"After your Jesus is stapled, then you may go *quietly* and *reverently* back to the table and use the red crayons to put blood on his hands and feet. Most of you have done this before, so remember how you did it and help our little guest. *Then*, when everyone is finished, we'll have refreshments."

You can't believe it. Jesus that came and took Grandma to Heaven like Superman flying down, and they beat him up and slam staples in like it's some fun project.

You're supposed to be working on your impulse control, but you move like a tornado, stomp up to the front in your tight, shiny shoes, grab both staplers and throw them across the room. You see the bloody red crayons on the table and push them off onto the floor.

They just stand there mean and stupid with their mouths hanging open. You rip Jesus off the cross Bossy Nancy is working on and tear out the staples.

Then you swoop around the table grabbing all the Jesuses. Katy Wilkins holds on to hers until it rips in half, but you pull the other half away from her and then demand all the others, doing a rescue operation like the U.S. cavalry in the cowboy movies on cable.

You're going to get Jesus away from all the mean little girls who like to push other people down on the playground and make them turn the rope forever but never let them jump.

"Gimme it! you're not gonna do all this mean stuff to Jesus. Gimme that one, too. You're nothing but a bunch of ignorant rednecks and to hell with your goddamn hellhole hick party! I want to call my mother to come take me home!"

The room gets very quiet after that. Pamela's mother just points with her long red fingernail to the desk in the corner where the telephone is. You wake them up from their nap, and then you go out and wait on the curb with the ten ripped and stapled Jesuses clenched in your hand.

When they come, they ask if something's wrong, but when you say the kids were mean, as usual, they pretty much lose interest, and you drive home in silence.

You look back as you drive off and see them all outside, staring at the car, the two mothers and all the children. You know what's going to happen. You're going to pay big time for this. What happened before will look like a vacation compared with what's coming.

When you get home, Mother and Daddy go back to their interrupted nap, not knowing anything about the phone calls that are coming. You go to your room and pull out all the staples, take Jesus off the crosses, scotch-tape the hands and feet back where they tore, cut the outstretched arms off at the shoulders and tape them back in a more comfortable position hanging at his sides. You know you're a neat paster and taper, and you look at the Jesuses with a happy feeling.

Then you pull open the bottom drawer that's all yours, where Mother never puts fresh clothes, that you have for your baby blanket and your dolls' clothes. You carefully lay all the Jesuses on nice soft dresses and cover them up with the baby blanket.

Then you see the picture of Grandma you keep on the top of your dresser, Grandma when she was alive, with her soft white hair and her flowered dress. You remember when you got to spend that week with her, sleeping in the little bed she put in her room when she knew you were scared of the dark.

You move the Jesuses apart, making sure all their parts stay together, so you can put Grandma in the middle, cover them up again and shut the drawer, softly, and there they stay entombed, radiating reassurance, until the day you unpack them to leave for college.

Diary

NO ONE BUT ME calls her Isabella. They just call her Sybil's clone, and I wasn't even supposed to be there, but I snuck in when Dr. Goodheart was talking to Mummy and Daddy, and I saw her.

I never said that I stayed there behind the curtain that day I met Isabella. She was just sound asleep in her jelly bed, but I went over close and smiled at her. Her eyes stayed closed, but I know she smiled a little bit at me and I told her I would never, never cut off her leg even if I lost mine.

At my school we all have clones. We learn about them in science. They're called our Genetically Paired Medical Auxiliaries.

The kids in public schools don't usually have clones. They sometimes get them when they're grown up, just in case, but they're not like ours that are exactly the same age as us.

When I was just a nursery school kid, I asked my mother if I could invite Isabella to my birthday party, but she said don't be silly, clones are not real people. They're just depots for medical purposes. Couldn't all the kids bring their clones, I said, like the nannies. They could have their own party like the nannies do.

But why, why, why, I asked. I tried for days, and cried, and even locked myself in my room. She's a little girl, just like me, I said, but they said it was impossible and could never be.

Ever since then, on my birthday, when the house is full of whispers and I find little snippets of gold paper and ribbons in Mummy's wastebasket, I think about Isabella. Oh, I don't mean

I think about her all the time, but on my birthday, our birthday, I never forget.

Today is my sweet sixteen party. I have a dress that's all white and floaty, and I'll have fresh flowers for my hair. The workmen are putting up a big canopy on the side lawn for dancing, and delivery trucks have been rushing in and out all day, but I have remembered Isabella lying there naked in her jelly.

I know a lot about clones now. I did them for my Science Fair project last year and got an Honorable Mention. I've learned to act casual about the whole subject so Mummy and Daddy don't stiffen up and act suspicious.

I guess I know now how silly it was to want Isabella to come to my party. Clones' minds are not awakened. They have never spoken. From the moment of their conception, they are drugged to sleep. Every day, machines rotate them, push their arms and legs up and down and around and around so that their muscle tone will be good when we need them.

If I want to, now that I am married, I can have Isabella carry my child. That way, I won't get stretch marks or saggy breasts. My husband will love me more if I stay beautiful. Secret thoughts whisper to me. Is it possible he will love Isabella more when she is big with his child? I must make sure he never sees her. It's not considered really nice, anyway, to see someone's clone. They say our clones always look younger than we do, and more beautiful. If science could transfer our brains, we could stay ever young and beautiful, moving to a younger body every few years.

When she is old enough to know, will my child yearn to see her birth mother? Will she love her more than me? There is no word in our language for the child of a clone. Auntie Isabella?

What will happen if I die? Will my husband come and take Isabella away to be my memorial? Will he take her from her bed of jelly and put her in my bed?

If I grow old and have kept my promise to Isabella, will she come to lie beside me in my walled crib and keep me warm?

The Notebook

I NO LONGER HEAR CONFESSIONS in the confessional with that comfortable assumption of anonymity but sit down with the penitent in my office, a crucifix beside us on a table. As a concession to shy souls, I keep the lights low and have the two comfortable chairs at an angle so we don't stare directly into each other's eyes. The sacrament of reconciliation, we call it now, a conversation about clearing away obstacles between ourselves and God.

Most come irregularly in the same way they get mass over with early on Saturday night, so they can party and sleep in on Sunday morning.

Not Miss Arpel. She was my late Thursday afternoon regular. By the time she came in, I would be tired, but I could pretty much let her small sins flow over me like sunshine at an outdoor cafe in Italy. Not that I didn't take her worries seriously, but it was not hard to absolve such gentle mistakes, eating too many sweets, irritation at a co-worker who didn't return her stapler, anger that her mother and father hadn't sent her to college.

The sacrament of reconciliation is not a social event but knowing the nature of Miss Arpel's sins and knowing that on Thursdays she came to confession directly from her day's work in an insurance company office, I had grown into the habit of having a cup of tea ready for her. Before the secretary left for the day, she would leave the cups and the hotpot ready in the window, saying, there, it's all ready for Miss Arpel. When I heard her light steps coming down the hall, I turned on the hotpot and could pour the tea shortly after her arrival.

Oh, it's so good of you, Father, she always said. I don't want to be under false pretenses, but somehow I've never said the secretary puts it out, says it's all ready for poor Miss Arpel. I'll take that little sin on my soul, and let her think there's someone in the world who'll put himself out a little for her, thinks she must be tired and needs a cup of tea.

On this particular Thursday, I sensed she seemed preoccupied. Perhaps it was the way she resisted sinking into the comfort of the chair or the way she kept her large purse on her lap instead of on the floor beside her. Maybe I was just picking up on something in her expression.

I made some conversation, as I always do, touched on the weather, unusually warm for Ash Wednesday the next week, my plans to take an early summer trip to Walsingham in England for a silent priests' retreat. She listened politely and nodded, but her smile was small and formal, not eager as it usually was.

My remarks came to an end, and there was one of those awkward silences. I began to say the words that would let her begin her confession, but this time, instead of being eager to begin, she opened her large purse and pulled out one of those black-and-white exercise books.

I've been coming to see you for a long time now, Father.

I've been in this parish for nine years now, Miss Arpel, and I think I've seen you every week.

Not quite. I've made my confession to you 465 times. It should be 468 but somehow I've missed three weeks. I remember I had that bad flu three years ago, and two times I went on a vacation tour. I always made an extra long confession after I came back.

I know you did, Miss Arpel. I remember those times well.

There was another silence and then, as if she were making a resolve, she said, I haven't been totally honest with you or God, Father. Yes, I have confessed to some sins, but there have been others that I could never bring myself to tell you.

She held the black-and-white notebook in the air and looked at me significantly.

Six thousand, seven hundred and forty-two.

Six thousand, seven hundred and forty-two?

Additional sins. Quite a lot for someone like me, unmarried, a steady churchgoer, a colorless, boring person. Wouldn't you say so?

What was I to say? What did she need me to say? Was she seeking honesty? If so, then I had to say to her, yes, you have led a quiet life, but a quiet life can have its own charms. I could be honest but add that much to soften it.

Your sins have not usually been large. Small sins, I would say, because your life has been quiet, which can be a blessing. You are very scrupulous.

What I have not faced in all these years is that while I have confessed what I might call, using the usual terminology, sins of commission, there are many things I have not done, yet should confess, what I call my sins of omission. Wrongful things I have wished to do. I would not like to die with these sins on my conscience. I have written those sins here, described in the fullest details, in this book. What I wished for, even if it was against the laws of God. I wrote these things down, went back, re-read them. I should not have done so. I have decided to leave this confession with you, until my usual time next week. Then you will tell me what I must do.

Then she stood and murmuring the usual pleasantries, I walked with her to the door, put the notebook in my briefcase and returned to the rectory. My housekeeper, who has served probably generations of priests in this parish, gave me hamburgers and cabbage before she left. I took a new bottle of wine, the food and watched the news before I switched to brandy and Miss Arpel's book of sin.

Each entry was dated but without the year. It took me a while to understand who Michael was.

The first entry. December 31. Michael has just left. After we knelt and said our prayers together, for the first time, we made love, in front of the fire, silent except for our sounds of passion and the fire snapping, logs falling. Our love matched the fire. He called me his bride. Afterward, as we lay in the warmth, my fire-warmed hair covered his chest. We had only time for a final glass of cabernet before he had to leave, to spend the last moments of the year alone with his God.

January 1. Such a long day. Michael was offering a special New Year's Mass but somehow I couldn't go. I was not yet ready to merge our private life and his public life as a priest of God. I filled my hot water bottle and got into bed naked. Slept and woke filled with longing, caressed myself while thinking of him. If only his hands had been the ones to satisfy my passion. A cup of tea with cream and sugar in the evening while watching the National Geographic special on the wounds of Christ.

And on and on. She had spent the last ten years living with me. We had had a child together. I had always seen through her thinness, her grey hair, her carefully mended, conservative clothing, to the loving woman inside. She had cooked me meals, written me poems, kept careful summaries of every sermon I had ever preached.

Now, for some reason, she was repenting. Not, I think, of the secret life but of the fact that she had never done anything to make it come alive. She had, I think, in her own mind lived a lie. Her life of churchgoer, altar guild, gardener, and, for a period of time, even Brownie Scout leader had no place in the black-and-white notebook, the life she had never had the courage to seize, not necessarily with me. I had simply been the convenient man. She would never, even in her dreams, have been a home-wrecker.

I poured another glass and thought of my own life. I, too, had had my other life, the one that, unlike her, I had always confessed. She had named our child Rose, and I had sometimes thought what it would be like to sit in front of a roaring fire with my child in my arms, explaining about God.

I put the notebook in my briefcase and contemplated the difficulty of getting up the stairs, a problem I seemed to have with increasing frequency. I'd make it, though. I always did. Tomorrow I'd call on Miss Arpel, call on her in her house, which I had never done, trust I would find the words to make her see her life had been justified, and her omissions not worthy of confession. They were just the alternative universes that let you get through life.

On impulse, I dialed her number although it was late. From the speed with which she picked up the telephone, I knew she had not been asleep. I hadn't thought this through, but somehow some good words came, and I told her I had read her notebook and felt very close to her now, that I understood and everything would be fine, whatever that meant. I said I would come to see her tomorrow, and we said goodbye. She sounded happy.

My room was cold. My bed was cold, but it seemed like too much trouble to go downstairs and open another bottle, and eventually I fell asleep, wondering if it had been the right thing to call her. At least it had let her get through the night.

She hadn't got through, however. We got word the next morning that Miss Arpel hadn't made it through the night. Her office had become alarmed and sent someone to check. It seems she had been suffering from heart problems for some time, and on that night her heart had just stopped. She had left money for her burial, and altar guild took care of the details.

So sad, isn't it, Father, having had such a drab life. She spent all her life here, always worked in the same office, never married, seldom went away on vacation, no children. I gather her family all passed before she did, years ago. She was all alone.

No, she wasn't, I thought and wanted to say, but she would't have wanted any explanations, not after keeping her love affair and her child secret all these years.

I preached her sermon cryptically, saying what she would understand and nobody else would. I told them all, the regulars who always came to a funeral for the lonely and forgotten, that sometimes those who seem quietest have very rich interior lives, and that as her priest, I could attest her interior life had been rich and full of love.

I told them I would take care of the tombstone and erected a small one, carved with roses, of pink granite, appropriate in every way for someone who had endured and made sweetness of deprivation.

What to do about the notebook was difficult. I couldn't throw it away to end up in a landfill. Ripping it apart? Equally unthinkable. I carried it in my briefcase until the night before Ash Wednesday.

That evening I usually built a little fire in the brazier I used only once a year. The people had retrieved blessed palms from last year's Palm Sunday, taken them out from whatever safe place they had been in, tucked behind a picture of the Sacred Heart, twisted into crosses that leaned against the dining room clock, coiled into a shape that would fit easily into a jewelry box, and left them in the church to be burned for the next year's Ash Wednesday—ashes for the foreheads of the faithful. Remember thou art dust and to dust thou shalt return.

I took the notebook and some brandy out to stay warm in the late afternoon chill, and as I stirred the fire, read a few of the entries again.

He wouldn't drink so much if we could be open about our love. Why can't I live with him? I'm of an age now it wouldn't cause talk. I could be his housekeeper. Have a nice meal ready at the end of the day, a warm dessert. Make the rectory a real home. Without saying anything about it, I could take little Rose along. She could run in and out and make everyone happy. The parish would be forgiving, not knowing her father, but knowing I'd chosen to have her rather than an abortion.

Then written in a different color of ink, in larger letters, bold and impetuous, she had added on last entry. I love you. I will love you forever.

I put the notebook on the fire and waited until it was consumed, then stirred it in with the palms. I will send Miss Arpel's love out on the foreheads of the parishioners, out into the world, to protect them for a little while from remembering that they come from dust and to lonely dust they will return. Just for a little while.

Those Who Go Up in Towers

GOD'S NOT GOING TO be mad at us. Jesus on the cross is our god, not theirs. They whipped him and killed him, treated him just like they did us, so believe me, he's going to understand.

Their god? Well, their god is fat. Self-satisfied. Their god doesn't bleed from a crown of thorns while everybody gives him a mock trial and makes fun of him. That's our god. Their god is made of brass. They build a fire in his belly and throw in newborn babies.

If you're sentenced to death when you're a kid, their god teaches them to wait until you're eighteen to execute you. Hell, their god knows how to twist a piece of skin on your arm until you give him your lunch money. Their god waits until you're getting a drink at the fountain and shoves your face down until your nose bleeds.

So we're not going to worry about what we have to do. Jesus will understand.

At least he had some happy years before they killed him. I don't ever remember being safe, even in kindergarten, that should be a place where you color. Have snacks. Learn to do stuff. Learn, that's the word. Not do stuff you know how to do already.

So I wasn't as quick as the other kids. So what? There's nothing wrong with that. The Bible says the last shall be first, but it's nothing *their* god would say. Fat chance. Just try being last. I learned the truth about that when I was five years old.

Like learning to print. I remember sometimes I'd work all morning getting my "A" just right. Nice straight lines. The crossbar at the right place, in proportion to the lines. You can put a lot of work into an A if you care about doing it right. So I'd ask the teacher to show me a few times. Nothing wrong with that, is there? Isn't that why teachers are there?

But they just want to show you one time, and then you do it. Well, you don't get it *right* going fast like that, do you? Maybe the other kids had a whole page of letters, but were they good? No. They were crooked, some big, some little, straggling over and under the lines. Maybe I'd just have one or two, but they were perfect. You'd think a teacher would respect someone who tried to do perfect work.

But guess who got locked in the room to keep making letters instead of going out for recess? Big deal. I didn't care. The teachers taught those snobby kids not to let me play, anyway. I liked being locked in. I took her stuff out of the desk and stomped on it. Pretended I was the boss, made all those kids stay in and write while I went out and played, had the whole playground, the swings, the slide, everything for myself. Those who laugh last laugh best. That's in the Bible, too.

Things weren't any better at home. I always slept too hard, couldn't get up to go to the bathroom, so I had accidents, okay? Just that, accidents. They were just accidents. You concentrate on doing everything right all day, you sleep hard.

But instead of helping me, maybe waking me up so I could go to the bathroom, *he* made me drink. I had to have a glass of water every half hour before bedtime and stay up really late until I was so tired I never woke up. Then after I had an accident, he made me lay on my wet bed while he whaled me and said I had to learn not to be a goddamned baby

Then he'd lock me in the closet all weekend, week after week. Nothing to eat, nothing to drink. It was hard after a while even to breathe. Once he kept me locked up like that for years. Alone in the darkness that never ended.

They kept picking on me at school, and *he* kept whaling me at home, but what could I do? When you're that age, it's hard to think of anything. I mean, you don't have access, do you? You can't get hold of a gun, and you're not strong enough to use a knife. But I'd learned about the Bible by then, and I learned where there's a will, there's a way.

So I thought, fire's easy. Even kids can get matches, and everything can be cleansed with fire. Like Sodom and Gomorrah that he read to me out of the Bible at bedtime.

I won't ever forget the first night I waited until I knew *he* was asleep, and then I went out the window, and I burned that school. Burned it to the ground. Another night I burned the teachers' houses. Then I burned the other students' houses, any places I knew. I'd sit in the shadows under the trees across the street while things burned up in red explosions, and the ambulances rushed in with their sirens screaming, and for a little while, I'd feel safe.

When they caught me, I thought, okay, here's my chance to explain. I thought they would be filled with horror. Comfort me. Take steps to make sure it didn't happen to anybody else. I told them how it all started in kindergarten, thinking they'd understand, but guess what, I just got punished again.

The Kindergarten Killer, that's what they called me, and sent me away to those places where they locked me in, and I couldn't breathe. I can't understand why nobody ever wanted to let me breathe.

When they take your breath, that's the worst.

That's when I learned about splitting us apart, making you and me, so one of us could go out and breathe for the other until punishment time was over. Sorry you were always the one got left, but I thought I would die if I couldn't get some air to breathe even though I had to leave you there in the room without windows.

The first time they wrapped me up in that horrible jacket with long long sleeves, I just sat there and screamed until I used up all the air, so I had to squirm to where the door was and lay on the floor in front of the crack where the air should have come through, but it didn't because there was all that thick padding. I didn't want to leave you, but I couldn't stay there anymore.

I just split off and went up on the top of the building where I could look down to where the people walked so far below they looked like ants. I breathed plenty of air and concentrated on sending enough back so you could breathe. I spent a lot of time there after that, just breathing.

When they came to let you out, I knew, and just slipped back inside instantly when they opened the door and let us out to where the air was if we promised to be good. After that first time, I went away whenever things got awful. That was the only way I could hold on to breathing.

But I wasn't as stupid as they always said, and I could see instantly there was stuff in that place that was going to be useful. Like therapy. I always enjoyed therapy when they taught us how to get in touch with our feelings, like that shrink said.

Make a fist, he said. Make it as hard and as tight as you can. Feel the tension. Hold it until it hurts. Then slowly release it. C'mon, let's do it together now. Make your whole arm tight. Hold it. Hold it. Hold it. Now, slowly, release it. Now tighten your shoulders.

Remember how we went through the whole body, from head to toes, learning to tighten with rage and then relax? Remember that? Now you know how it feels to be relaxed, he said. You can come to that place whenever you need to feel relaxed. Just work up your rage and then let go of it.

Yeah, I smiled and agreed it was a good thing to know, except for the letting go part, but I didn't tell him that. I really enjoyed learning what he said, but all the time I was laughing inside, thinking how I was going to use it, and if they knew, they'd just say I was stupid again, but I was getting smarter than any of them.

Most of the time, things got worse and worse, and finally that time came, remember, when they wrapped me in ice-cold wet sheets and forced a gag between my teeth, said how this was going to help me, and then the electrical whipping began. I never imagined something like that, never in my life.

I tried to run, tried to hide, fought, but there were too many of them. One, that big bastard who looked like my father, especially laughed when he held me down while I was struggling. Laughed because he knew what he was doing, liked doing it. It wasn't any use, in the end. They always won, time after time.

No matter how hard I tried to resist, I ended up in the wet bed, strapped down, and then the whip came over and over and over, and I had to fight and fight to get air but nobody paid any attention.

So I had to just go away, but I could still hear you screaming, and so I stood in the corner and made my body tight with rage like the therapist showed me, preparing for some day when I would be strong enough for revenge, made it tight with rage but never let go. Finally, we just sort of separated forever, and I couldn't get back inside.

Now it's okay, isn't it? We're like twins, except one of us can be seen, and the other one can't. Now I'm going to explain to you slowly and carefully what I learned when they were whipping us, and they're never going to hurt us again.

Understand this: it's all right to want justice. Revenge, when you didn't start anything, when they all did it to you, is a natural desire to restore the balance of the universe. This is how the last get their turn to be first, as the Bible says. The Bible gives you a lot of good advice, but it doesn't always tell you exactly how to do it, so it took me a long time to figure this out.

I'm going to teach you so you don't have to learn it on your own. I won't get angry and shut you up no matter how long it takes. I'll explain over and over again, in a calm, gentle voice, until you can do it yourself without even thinking about it. This is what they taught me, all of them, with their wet sheets and their whips, when they laughed at me and locked me up and took all my air away.

Okay. Think about wanting something as hard as you've ever wanted anything in your life. Remember how much you wanted food and water when you'd been locked in the closet for days? Remember? Remember how there wasn't enough air to breathe, so you lay down on the floor and put your mouth close to the crack under the door and thought about being outside in a storm where you could suck in big gulps of clear, fresh air? Remember?

Remember how your body and soul used to scream for some-one to hold you and say nice things, but everybody just laughed at you or ripped your clothes off and threw you down? Remem-ber how angry you felt after a while of wanting just those easy, everyday things everybody else took for granted and how when you tried to get them, they put you on that icy wet bed and whaled you?

Now imagine your whole mind and body wanting revenge just that much. Go to your right fist. Clench it. Go on, do it. Feel the adrenaline surge through your body. Feel your muscles like burning steel bands. Stay that way. Now clench your arms. Make them like solid pieces of burning iron. Now your neck and head. Brace them, clench them. Now your torso, your neck, your legs. Your whole body is tense with rage, solid as rock, filled with hatred. Hold on to that feeling.

Whenever you need strength for revenge, you can come back to this feeling. This anger is always there, waiting. But don't let your face or your body *show* what you're doing. To all outward appearances, you must be a calm and relaxed person, walking around, sitting quietly in a chair, making small talk, stuff like that. Only underneath, they'll be there, iron-hard, fiery, mus-cles of hate.

This is what I learned in those places where there was no light and no love and no air. Maybe I remember it better than you because a lot of the time I was outside, and you were just trying to breathe. I'm sorry about that, but now it's your turn, too.

We have to conceal our feelings until the correct time, but that time is coming soon. This is the last day. We're out now, we can lock our door, and there's always enough air to breathe. Everyone compliments us and says how well we're doing. They nod approvingly, and we smile and thank them.

All the time, inside, think about a red balloon. Blow it up. Fill it with your rage. It begins to look like the stupid fat red faces of everybody who tortured you. Remember, maybe you're out now, but they're just waiting to get you and do it all over again. Never forget that! Now, imagine sticking the balloon with a pin. It explodes and rains fire over their stupid laughing faces that don't give a damn you can't breathe. Pretty soon they're dead, and you feel relaxed and powerful.

Think you've got it? Good. As the Bible says, now we are ready to bind and loose.

Tomorrow is the day. We'll find a high place where there's lots of people, maybe a church tower or the top of one of those stupid business buildings in Center City. Climb up to the top. Make sure no one is around. If anyone comes, we'll pretend we're admiring the view. Maybe a camera would be a good idea. Pretend we're taking pictures.

But then, when we're alone, we'll take the rifle out and assemble it. Then we'll go to the place where retribution lives and turn into iron-hard instruments of flaming justice.

Far below, the enemy will come with their stupid fat red faces So many of them. They are the people who twist skin and take lunch money, they sentence people to rooms without any air, they stand there and laugh. Those are the ones we are going to kill.

But there will be others among them. We have to be careful not to shoot them. They're the ones like us. We have to keep them safe, the ones walking quietly, hoping not to be noticed, not to be bullied, not to be locked up.

You'll know them when you see them. They'll be walking on the edges of the sidewalk, carrying little paper bags with their sandwiches for lunch, not walking off to fancy restaurants. They'll step off into the grass when the powerful ones with fat red faces come by.

These are the ones we have to protect, and we'll know them. When we begin the cleansing, they'll look up at us as the red balloons explode into the landscape. We'll let them run into safe places as the enemies die.

We have to remember to save the last bullets for us. If they get us, they'll lock us up again in the closets where we can't breathe, they'll put us on the wet beds and make fun of us as the whips come down. This is our only chance, and we can't make a mistake.

But if we do this well, the others will remember us in their prayers, bless us and keep our names alive. There's no need to be afraid.

Remember. We didn't do anything wrong. We're just going to be up there with the *good* god, up there with the sun, looking down into the valley. Into shadows, that's all. The shadows of the valley of death, where the dry bones live with their fat red faces and their whips, down there among the buildings. Soon they'll all be dead, *they'll* be the bones, *they'll* be the ones can't breathe anymore.

But *we'll* be up there with the *good* god. We'll be safe. Until more of them come through the door with their whips and their cold wet sheets to make fun of us like they did before. We can't let that happen.

After they're all dead, see, we can sit up there for a little while and breathe the fresh air. It's always nice and comfortable to rest after you've done a good day's work. But that good time won't last forever. After cleansing everything down below with clean bright flames, we'll have to use the two bullets left so we won't ever be separated again.

Pretty soon we'll hear voices and sirens. We'll know that's the time to say good-bye. But everything will be all right. This time we'll go away together. To where the *good* god has lots of nice fresh air for us, and this time they won't be able to whip us apart, ever again. We won't even be as lonely as you and me, just one.

The two of us become one again, breathing soft and easy, as much air as we want, forever and ever.

Airdwellers

MOST OF THE FOLKS around here still live in all these old row-houses been here since the rich people moved out in the nine-teenth century, but more and more of us, the ones that's lost their homes to so-called Urban Renewal, well, we just live . . . up in the air.

That's right. In between the old houses you still see stand-ing, the city comes with wrecking balls and men and trucks and takes our homes away. Ceilings, walls, floors . . . everything, just like they took mine.

I moved what I could out on the sidewalk—my couch and chairs. Kitchen table. Refrigerator and radio. Candy dishes and hairdriers and clothing. Moved it out right across the street, and then I and the children and the neighbors sat there eating lemon frappe water ice while I watched the walls of my home come tumbling down.

About a day, that's all it took. First they ripped out the floor on the ground level so you could see all the way down to the basement. Then they filled that up with the walls, ceilings, and the rest of the floors. See? Didn't even have to haul anything away. Saved the city money.

My neighbor, old Mrs. Zervas, in her usual morning costume of fiercely starched print dress and calico cobbler's apron, sat on the straightest kitchen chair she could find (so as to mortify the flesh, I expect) and fanned herself with her famous hand-painted fan. Her sailor son brought it back from Japan, and she thinks it's worth a queen's ransom, but I expect it's the Japanese equivalent of junk from the dollar store. Well, she went on and on.

"A wonder indeed! Take away the air, and a basement can hold a house. Oh, the vanity of worldly things."

We just talked past her the way we always do and sat there throughout the day. I watched my home disappear and it hurt. After the first half hour, the kids lost interest and went off to play kick the can. I must say, the neighbors took it in turns to sit with me, and commiserate, and along about suppertime laid out a nice meal of fried chicken, potato salad, coconut cake and iced Coca Cola.

With all my good stuff sitting out there in that neighborhood, I wasn't going to leave, so I just sat there throughout the night, after using Lorrie Beacham's bathroom for a spit bath and a good dusting of Johnson's baby powder. The children thought it was fun to curl up on the couch and on blankets draped across two kitchen chairs pushed together. Tyrone and LeRoy, my two oldest, shared a mattress on Molly Johnson's porch.

The next morning, when the dust had died away, you could see the memory of my stairsteps and rooms outlined in brick and plaster on the walls of the adjacent houses. Although there weren't any floors, walls or ceilings left, our neighborhood is way down there under the poverty level, and we're used to living on air.

I hired that shiftless Taylor boy for his muscles and between him, myself, and the children, we carried all the furniture back up, set it in place, and carried on with our lives. Pretty much.

There was nothing we could do about the plumbing, so we had to rely on the charity of neighbors and the McDonald's down the street.

Electricity wasn't so hard. You can always borrow a little electricity from a neighbor. Mr. McIlhenny from the airhouse up one and over two blocks was an electrician for the city before he retired, and he's always glad to oblige if you get the materials. Still, some of the folks who still live in traditional houses of bricks and wood looked down on those of us living in open air. The kids got upset.

One day I sent Leola to get a dollar's worth of cheese and lunch meat down to Mrs. Espada's corner store, and she started in on Leola.

"You couldn't get me to live in one of them airhouses. Why, you forget to pull things up for a week or two, and one morning you're gonna wake up in that vacant lot down below. In this world, that's taking your life in your hands. You hear what I'm saying, girl? You tell your mama to get on a schedule, or sure as shootin' you'll end up in the family way before you're fifteen."

Well, as you can imagine, Leola came home upset. "Mama," she said, as I put Miracle Whip on a piece of bread and artistically arranged a slice of lunch meat before smothering it with another piece of bread.

"Mrs. Espada says that airhouses keep sinking and hardly anyone can keep them up. She says we might end up in the lot if we're not careful to keep pulling ourselves up."

Then her little voice started to wobble.

"I might wake up to find a crack dealer in my bed and I'll have to drop out of eighth grade and have a baby."

She put her sandwich on my well-scrubbed table and began to wail like her heart was gonna break. A car slowed down and the occupants looked over in alarm, but seeing only Leola bawling, went on before they even saw the rude gesture I made at them.

Well, I just took off my apron and threw it down in the air where the kitchen floor used to be, took my daughter by the hand and, nicely judging where the steps were by the marks on the wall, veritably marched us down the stairs and up to Espada's Corner Grocery, Fresh Meats and Vegetables, Hispanic and Caribbean Specialties, Food Stamps, and Women, Infants and Children's Program Accepted.

I let the screen door crash against the wall and it just stayed there, the spring not having functioned for some years.

That woman's eyes widened and her mouth opened in pure terror when I marched in and banged my hand on the counter.

"Never, never has anyone come to my house and not found the table scrubbed and the floor swept. In my house, greens are not cooked from a can and carrots are scraped."

I stared her down and turned to take care of the onlookers.

"Not for me the tumble-dry, the wash and wear. Never are we on the street not starched and ironed. Pulling ourselves up! Phooey! To me . . ." I watch TV, I have a sense of drama. I paused a moment, swept the store with my eyes, including those peering in from the sidewalk, ". . . to me, that is nothing! Daily, mind you, daily and more, shall we pull ourselves up! I invite you not to avert your eyes from my domicile as you walk past, and if you ever see us sinking one inch, I will eat my words!"

And I charged out of there with attitude. I was holding Leola's hand and walking so fast that poor girl was almost horizontal. When I got home, I ran up those airstairs.

"You, Tyrone, LeRoy, Leola, come help me. Germaine, you can help, too, honey, there's some little things you can help with. Leave baby Anthony alone. He's too little."

I'm telling you, we tugged everything up so high that the roofline, had we been so fortunate as to have one, would have been at least ten inches over the neighbors'.

I didn't stop there. The next morning, I sent them all out to play, and I turned that place out from top to bottom. I aired, I dusted, I scrubbed. You've gotta understand about air houses. You might think housekeeping would be easy when you don't have to wash windows, wax floors, but if some chores disappear, others need extra time.

Take clothes, for instance, when they're hanging in invisible closets. You know those tangles of shoes and old sneakers— you've all got them, you know what I'm talking about—that you could shut the closet door on?

Well, when your lives are up in the air, they've all got to be lined up neatly, *with* their soles sponged clean. And take beds. I like unmade beds that look like piles of whipped cream when you come back home tired and just want to dive in. Not in an airhouse. Unh-huh. You have to make every one of those beds every day.

You gotta wash every dish as soon as you use it. Imagine folks looking up and seeing you living there with all those spaghetti-smeared plates! *And* in cold water. We ran our water out of the

Lattimers' apartment, through a garden hose out the window, but for what I can paid, they wouldn't let us attach to the hot.

On the other hand, there ain't no floors to wash and wax, ain't no walls to keep clean of fingerprints, ain't no cobwebs to swipe down with a peacock feather, and, on the whole, except for a lack of privacy, I'm not sure I wouldn't trade in a walled house for an airhouse any day.

Every time I paid the man the half-rent under the table—that's what airdwellers have to pay—I felt pretty good. Put the other half away in cold cash at the bottom of my big black purse.

We got used to it. On Sundays, I still dressed up in my white deaconess dress, and when I heard the bell of the Good Humor truck, I knew it was time for me to head toward the Old Ship of Zion. That truck is Elder Zervas' chief source of income during the week, but on Sundays it calls the faithful to worship in the first floor of the Zervas house, where the living room serves as the Sanctuary, and the dining room, adjacent to the kitchen and its 30-cup coffee urn, as the Fellowship Hall.

I never missed a day of church, even when they changed my home from a regular house to an air house. Choir rehearsals, revivals, baptisms, and funerals—you could count on me. When I'm feeling low, I put my trust in the Lord and keep up my spirits by counting my blessings, even about air houses.

I admit maybe I was laying it on a little too thick that day I made my speech during the Fellowship Hour.

"For surely we are closer to the Lord!" I said. "What are prayers but air that we manipulate with our lips and tongues into shapes pleasing to God? Without a dirty old roof, covered with tar wherein are trapped the bones of innocent birds like the dinosaurs in the tar pits of old, long before the blessing of Adam and Eve to bring us our green peace, without the mockery of glass that prayers fight to get past, without the odors of grease and Lysol crippling their flight, my prayers spring as light and free as doves into the clarity of Heaven."

That's how I felt, and if Mrs. Zervas wanted to stomp off without even waiting for the coffee and buns we always have after the service, I figured that was her business.

In the beginning, we all spent a lot of time on the ground floor with its distant underpinning of solid rubble from the old house. The children, who had never been to Florida to watch underwater life from a glass-bottomed boat, all had favorites among the rats that made their homes in the mysterious nooks and crannies of our former roof and walls.

There were soft, grey mother rats with all their little naked pink babies and father rats, stalking around like they owned the place, and scaredy ones that just sort of skulked around the edges, moving aside when any of the others came around. A lot like people.

Each of the kids had their special rat. They watched it, dropped it tidbits, called little pet names to it until they began to trespass through the airfloors, acting like there weren't any barriers. You couldn't blame them. They smelled bread and cheese, taco chips and dip, not to mention Colonel Sanders leftovers.

The problem was they started to get real aggressive. Snapped the kids' Tastykakes right out of their hands. Finally, with the aid of the children and the muscular Taylor boy, I carried the first floor furniture up one more flight of airstairs and just abandoned the first floor, including the kitchen, to those pesky vermin.

After that, I still cooked, but everything that made a kitchen a kitchen had gone with the city truck or been thrown into the basement. We saved the refrigerator, but after several efforts to get it up the airstairs, we had to abandon it on the ground floor. On the second night after we retreated to higher ground, a truck pulled up in the dead of night, and I saw two men load it up. They couldn't see me. If I had turned on the electricity, they would have seen us all in our sleeping garments. I shouted for them to go away, but they just laughed like the silly asses they were.

"We'll be back for the sofa and chairs when they come down," one of them shouted and I shouted "Never!" but I think I was drowned out in the roar of their exhaust.

Well, I had to cook with a hot-plate, a Crock-Pot, and a cubic-foot refrigerator, all of which were easy to carry up and keep tugged up, and I made damn good food, if I do say so myself. Warm cornbread baked in a Dutch oven on the hot-plate. Stir-fried mushrooms gathered in Fairmount Park. Fresh-snapped string beans flavored with bacon. Chicken dipped in milk and flour and fried to a turn. Pigeons, too young to have diseases, swooped up in my butterfly net as they flew through the house. Beans simmered slowly with molasses and onions. All the delectable salads that a head of lettuce and innumerable wild greens from the park could yield. Cooking up in the air, with the rich smells causing up-turned faces from all passers-by, I kept my pots sparkling and wore a clean white apron every day, cooking for the world to see, like a television chef.

Still, more and more, I had to coax the kids to eat. They began to look definitely peaky, as Mrs. Zervas had of course pleas-antly observed at the Old Ship of Zion, where the old bitch, for-give me, Jesus, but there ain't no other way to put it, changed to another Sunday School class that I didn't lead.

I cajoled. I coaxed, finally shouted in desperation.

"You have to eat! Soon you will be nothing but bundles of skin and bones!"

Nothing helped. I used the ultimate threat.

"I will have to take you to the clinic!"

Nothing worked. They smiled, filled their plates, and pushed the food from one side to another, taking an occasional tiny taste.

I saw what was happening. Living in an airhouse, they were starting to eat airfood. They spoiled their appetites every day, dawdling home in the evenings, greedily sucking in smells of the neighbors' tantalizing dinners as appetizers, and then loll-ing contentedly on their beds as the more-satisfying-than-eating smells from the solid houses on either side of them combined into one gigantic burst of airfood.

They didn't even want to watch television. I tried to bribe them. Popped corn, offered candy bars when it was time for their favorite programs.

"No thanks, Mom. I can hear it just fine from here in my bed. Don't want to get fat from popcorn and candy. I'm fine, just fine," echoed from four other languid throats. "Fine, fine, fine, fine. . . ."

I coaxed. They ate tiny mouthfuls. I made miracles of French toast, pot roast, fresh rolls. Their lunch bags were crammed to bursting with portable buffets of tempting treats, but the day came when I just had to face it. They were wasting away. We had to go to the clinic.

I ironed my flowered two-piece and my hat, polished the shoes that looked so good and hurt my feet, got the children starched and ironed like they were going to Sunday School. Then there was the subway and two buses to the clinic and many hours in those very uncomfortable molded chairs in bright colors—you know the ones?—until a medical intern had time to see us, and then he said, "Why, these children are starving, neglected. Their very lives are in danger. How did this happen?"

I had planned what to say all through the hours of preparation and waiting, anticipated saying (but of course I didn't) *you, with your fine education and your gold Cross pen, you are not better than I! Child of old money, I doubt that you are stronger and smarter than this daughter of old poverty. My children are clever and tender. Don't judge them by their hanging heads and small replies. Because I present a card for payment instead of crisp green money or shining plastic, I am not a dumb animal. I understand your language and you do not understand mine. You don't speak better than I because my words are soft, and yours are clipped and hard. Not only do I understand you, I understand the insinuated words and tones you offer to your fellows. If I say this, you will punish me. I fear you.*

"I offer them food, sir. Chicken and rice, greens, even pineapple upside-down cake. . . . They do say, sir" (permit me a mild, shy boast), "that of all the airdwellers, I am the best cook. But my children have lost their appetites and eat only the food of the air, alas, the food of witchery. For my good solid food they have no appetite."

When I said that, the young doctor looked up at me. "You're one of those airdwellers? Well, of course the children are not doing well. You can't live with children in a place like that. No floors, no walls, no roof. There's no protection. It's not possible."

As he looked at my clean, well-dressed children clinging to my hands, he hesitated.

"It's . . . not even legal, you know." He made notations on the pad of paper he carried, wrote at length.

Oh, no. I thought of ripping the paper from his hands, vaulting the counter to remove all traces of papers with our names, but I have lived long enough to be wise in the ways of the world. I only took the prescription and thanked him.

Ah, how I regretted that I had not gone to a private doctor and paid from the saved rent money. Danger threatened hugely now. It was true. Airdwellers, technically homeless, are not supposed to receive even their checks from the government. The mail carrier had been kind, leaving the check for me as long as I was on the street waiting for it, but the authorities would consider me of no fixed address, an unfit mother, and only three months' worth of half-rents in my big black purse.

Yet it was true, I thought that night after the children had been tucked into their beds. We are meant to be dwellers on earth, not in the sky. Even birds, blessed with wings, touch the earth, sleep in a nest in a tree whose roots stretch deep down into moist darkness. There is no creature that lives in the way I am making my children live, in the air. I know that I am more and more tired, and now that the children have less energy, I must pull the house up all by myself.

The preceding week had been—I am leveling with you—very hard. We had been living in the air house all summer. I had begun to air the blankets, quilts, and afghans against the winter, thanking my lucky stars I had washed everything last spring and put them away clean. With a bright, fresh day to make the bedding fluffy and sweet-smelling, there was little else to prepare for the chilly air of autumn.

I went up to the roof and tied a line from one neighbor's chimney stack to an old leaning antenna. After I trudged up with load after load of bedding, I stood in the fresh air and laughed aloud to see the blankets fill big-bellied with wind like the sailing ships of old, becoming sweet for my children's nests.

But all for nothing. All the work and tugging, the cleverness, the planning. Now all to no purpose. The authorities will come. The social agency will come to pull the children away from me if necessary. If I throw myself under the wheels of their car, they will still take them away.

I could not sleep, sat awake the night through, thinking, with the shiny black purse tucked under my arm. Toward morning, I went to my cooking place, where a yellow book hung on a nail, and I filled the rest of the night with the useful information reliably found in the Old Farmer's Almanac, searching through symbols and recipes until I rejoiced, yes, rejoiced, at the chart with the phases of the moon. There was enough time. The trip to the clinic had been on Friday. They could not possibly come for the children before Monday. Two days, and two days until the fullness of the moon. There was time enough.

As the milky first light spilled from the sky, I woke them, ignored their sleepy reproofs.

"No, you must get out of your beds today and come to help me with the marketing. I have many things to buy this time."

They walked behind me as I marched through the store, pulling the wire marketing cart behind me, my good black purse firmly under my arm. In the beginning they complained a little but soon danced in excitement as purchase after extravagant purchase packed down in the cart.

Ah, the reassurance of that reserve of money. I bought a hammer with a large assortment of nails, a large package of needles with plenty of thread. A dozen lined tablets and a whole box of Ticonderoga #2's. How could I get school books? There was no way, but I bought a dictionary and a one-volume *Works of William Shakespeare*.

A pencil sharpener. A saw and an axe and a large roll of rope. Many boxes of matches. A large survival knife with a compass, fish hooks, and a tourniquet. An impressive and comforting first-aid kit in a white metal box with a big red cross. That was Saturday.

On Sunday, we made two trips to the supermarket and came home with twenty pounds of potatoes, ten pounds of rice, large bags of flour and cornmeal, bottles of vitamins, dry milk, and peanut butter. The children, delighted with the spending of so much money, slyly tipped in candy bars and boxes of cookies, which I pretended not to see. In the times ahead, a person might need a little familiar comfort for a while. For myself, it was several cans of good strong chicory-laden coffee.

The shopping took all of Saturday and Sunday, many trips up and down the airstairs, but finally I had everything stashed away in aircupboards and in every drawer, nook, and cranny I could find. Before I was finished, I had to go back two times for more rope and jugs of milk, which I emptied and refilled with water. Fortunately, Mrs. Espada's Corner Grocery was only one block away.

"Quite a shopping spree," said Mrs. Espada avidly, poking and hinting. Mrs. Zervas checked out everything in the cart as she pretended to be comparing two brands of canned corn, but I just gave them a big wide smile and sailed out of the store, my cart once again heavy with bags.

I put the jug filled with milk in the picnic cooler, ran a rope through the handles of the other nine, and anchored the rope to the frame of my bed. Anything that didn't have a secure place was bundled and tied down.

"Mama, why are all the things tied down? What are you doing?"

"Never you mind just now. But I wouldn't be surprised if we weren't going on a vacation for the first time in our lives."

After everything was secure, I sat down in the living room and showed them the possibilities. From the bright new atlas, they looked at the fresh orange groves of California, the dancers of Bali, the deserts of Morocco. The brochures glittering with adventure from the travel agency lay in gay profusion.

"But where are we going?"

"Doesn't matter. Anyplace is better than here."

"But what's the world like?"

I pulled them up so they were standing beside me and together we surveyed the sky. The moon was indeed full, filling the sky over our airy home.

"It's wonderful. Full of milk and honey. You can live off the fat of the land. Come."

I piled their arms with clean blankets and sheets, all the fresh laundry I had watched whipping in the wind on the roof. As they watched, I tied ropes to the four corners of each piece and anchored the ropes to the kitchen table, the bed, the bureaus. The children giggled and clutched one another as the house began to whip and buck in the tugging wind. I tied blanket after blanket that slowly filled, and the house began to lift.

"Hold on to each other, my children! Hold on to me! Your mother has not ever let you down, and now you must not be afraid!"

For the first time in a long long time, I felt giddy with excitement, like a young girl with her first lover. Knowing I was happy and strong, pretty soon the children lost their fearful faces, and we slowly cleared the adjacent houses.

The only moment of danger came as we veered dangerously low near the church steeple and, regretfully, I decided to push the couch overboard. As it fell end over end to the street, I watched, a little worried, to see if it hit anyone.

Only a lone Cadillac screeched safely to a halt as the couch thudded down in front of it, and the glittering occupants, all dressed up in their fancy opera clothes, emerged to stare up in amazement as we went on our way, me, a mother gilded by the moon, and my beautiful luminous children, all drenched in light, sailing across the dark blue night-time sky.